The Reset

A zombie apocalypse is here, but figuring out how to survive in the immediate aftermath is only the first step.

Elaine is just an ordinary woman, but when the apocalypse occurs, she must find a way to survive in an increasingly hostile world. Enter Liam, the policeman who saves her at their first meeting and provides assistance as they try to cope with the zombie outbreak brought about by an unknown infection that's spreading out of control.

Together they form a community, trying to save as many lives as they can, a place where people can be safe. Even in the throes of disaster though, emotions creep up, taking both of them by surprise. Who knows? They might just get their happy ever after...if they can survive.

I Dream of Zombies

After the apocalypse the world was a different place. Those who survived did so by wits, strength and by banding together.

Julia is a soldier—not by choice but circumstance in a world where taking up arms is a necessity. She's buried the softer parts of herself including her heart.

Leroy on the other hand is a warrior. An ex-soldier who has to come to terms with what he hides and a loner by choice.

Now they have a mission—retrieve those missing from *Camp Queanbeyan*. Survival is just the first step on a rocky road toward redemption and there's no guarantee of success.

Six Million Dollar Zombie

What do you get in the middle of a zombie apocalypse when you mix Canberra, a Priest and Kindergarten teacher?

Sparks. Lots of red-hot sparks of passion.

Dove may be a priest, but he's also a man and he's been alone for a long time. Rescuing Leonie by the side of the road is just the first step on a journey no one expected to love.

Leonie is running. Her family is gone, the zombies are chasing her, and she's rescued by a priest on a motorbike and taken to a community which welcomes her.

Life should only get better, but the forces who began the apocalypse are building an army of mutated, super-strong zombies. They plan to overtake everything those in the communities have built.

Times are only going to get tougher until they can defeat those with no interest in survival.

Make Room For Zombies

The Zombie Invasion—a failed government experiment—continues to spread...

When Adrienne makes the decision to pack up her infant twins, Leanne and Fiona, and make for an island, she has no idea just how much her life will change. The young widowed mother of two-month-old twins can't stay where she's been, because they're demanding more than she can give. They need her to be a warrior—something she isn't. The only option is to run to the idyllic island off the coast of Queensland.

The island might be cut off from the mainland with just one fortified bridge, but Jack knows it won't take much for the zombies to invade. With a half baked plan to blow up the bridge and the self-proclaimed mayor missing in action, he doesn't really need more responsibility.

That is until he meets Addie and the babies. Now, he's got so much more at stake than just the islanders protection. He's got a ready made family, if they can just survive the next few weeks.

Only time will tell, especially when zombies are involved.

THE ZOMBIOLOGY NOVELS

MAKE ROOM FOR ZOMBIES

A ZOMBIOLOGY NOVEL

Imogene Nix

No author is an island and in this instance, I've needed assistance from a professional with regards to the demolition of the bridge.

A huge thank you must go to Aaron (my on-call engineer), who answered questions he never thought he'd be asked (mainly about the best way to demolish a bridge without explosives.)

I've learned more about engineering and physics than I ever expected in this book!

Thank you also to my family for their understanding, to my handy-dandy editor Sassie and my lovely cover designer Fantasia Frog/Spittyfish Designs.

Thank you to my wonderful reader group who keep me going by constantly asking for more!

Lastly thanks to you, lovely reader, for purchasing my book.

If I could ask one last favour, it's remember to leave a review of the story.

Imogene Nix
Kingaroy
2021

<u>**Please note:**</u>

The UK and USA share the English language, but there are many words that are spelled differently. Some words have extra letters in the British spelling, such as the word cancelled. In American English, it is spelled canceled. There also words that interchange the letters c or s and sometimes z. For example, in America, you spell offense and in Britain, it is written as offence. We also use the letter u in many words, such as colour and flavour. These spellings are **not** incorrect.

We also have alternative words. Nappy, for example, is used in place of diaper and these are not incorrect terms, simply those appropriate in an Australian setting.

Also, please note:

Local Government is the term used in Australia to describe a City Council or Municipal Authority and is considered the third tier of government.

This book is written in UK English to reflect my Australian/English background.

PROLOGUE

Adrienne Goolem kept up the pace, her ancient car reliable though not beautiful, rolled along the pitted asphalt, dodging the wrecks here and there. In the backseat, she could see the twins, Leanne and Fiona, sleeping the day away.

"Keep at it," she muttered. The worst and most dangerous time were yet to come.

The fuel gauge was moving close to red, and she knew she'd soon have to find somewhere to fill up. It meant stopping. Getting out of the car…

Leaving the babies unprotected.

But what other option is there? No, she'd have to chance it. There's no way she'd reach her destination without that last top up.

A dilapidated sign ahead beckoned. Carefully she angled the vehicle in, up against the bowser, and took a moment to look.

Quiet.

She turned off the engine, waiting another heartbeat. Eyes scanning wildly, looking for signs of shuffling creatures.

Adrienne tugged the keys from the ignition and slid out. "Stay here. Stay quiet," she murmured to the sleeping babies.

She ran now, around the back of the car, slipping open the cover and snatching up the nozzle, hoping like hell it was unlocked.

The fuel sputtered out, and she gave silent thanks, shoving it into the tank, hearing the thrum as it flowed.

When the handle clicked, she shoved it back, reached into her pocket for a note, and slid it under the rock before closing the lid and running back to the door. She, like many others, had taken to leaving money out on the bowsers. Who or if anyone collected it, well, that was a matter for the owners, wasn't it? At least she'd done the right thing.

She slid into the seat, inhaling deeply, and closed the car door. Not a second too soon either, as the dirge she knew well filled the air. It terrified her, because she knew what would show itself all too soon.

The engine sputtered when she tried to start the car, then died. Her blood pressure spiking. So much at stake. It wasn't just her, but two innocent babies in the backseat. "Come on," she entreated, feeling the sting of tears, and tried once more. This time the engine caught.

On a whispered 'thanks', Adrienne—or Addie, as anyone who'd known her before the plague called her—steered the car onto the road, letting the thunder of pumping blood and organ settle back into a usual rhythm.

When she'd set out for the island, it had been with the knowledge she was leaving the relative safety of the hospital behind. For a settlement only whispered of by other survivors.

All she knew for certain was that the long bridge between the island and the mainland was going to be severed. Keeping their ability to get back to the mainland by boat. "I can live with that," she told herself.

Whatever it took to protect the two in the backseat.

They were all she had left.

***

Jack looked at the bridge. "And when do you want me to drop two sections?" The long, nearly kilometer stretch that joined them to the island was an imposing structure of concrete. He still thought the plan was as crazy as the first time he'd heard it two weeks ago.

"As soon as possible. Our temporary fencing is doing the job for now, but the creatures are becoming more focused on reaching the island. Yesterday, Tommy shot one who made it through the first barrier." The self-proclaimed mayor shook his head. He was the councilor for the island region and the most senior elected person locally to survive the initial wave. "Said he was a huge bugger."

Stripping his boots and socks, he made his way onto the soft sand and squatted, looking up. "It's not going to be easy. Those girders up there? They're huge and solid concrete. Not going to be easy to move. I've got to work out what we have that will do the job, Sir. I might be an engineer, but it's got to be safe and effective. Not half-assed."

The man gasped like a fish. "But—"

"If I'm going to ask people to risk their lives, I need to minimize those risks. They aren't dispensable."

The mayor harrumphed and Jack turned away, heading for the road.

At the car, he brushed the sand clinging to his feet, slid on his socks and shoes and climbed into the car, waiting for the mayor to follow. "If there're any drawings at the office, I'll have a better idea. I need to think, chat to my guys. See what equipment we can come up with."

The car slid away from the curb, smoothly, as Jack considered the situation they now found themselves in. The country abandoned by the world. Small enclaves of safety springing up here and there. As a result, safety, availability of foods and healthcare had become priorities.

Being the only engineer on the island, a lot of the infrastructure issues had fallen on his shoulders. He needed to ensure there was a long-term plan for water and sewerage. Investigate ways to boost and maintain the electrical infrastructure, while also stopping further incursions of zombies onto the island. Not much. He had to hold back the snort that rose.

"Drop me off here," the mayor demanded as they came upon the police station. "I have a meeting with the Sargent next."

Jack pulled over and waited for the portly man to clamber from the car, beads of sweat rolling down his face; heaving a sigh of relief as the mayor tottered inside the building. Not that he didn't like the man, it was just that the guy didn't understand the realities of Jack's job.

"And if, by some chance, we do once again form a united government, then we could all become accountable for our actions." *No, I won't take shortcuts. Whatever I do, I'll make sure to do it right.*

CHAPTER 1

Abandoned vehicles dotted the entrance to the bridge, and even worse, rats and rabid dogs circled certain vehicles. Looking too closely wasn't in her plan.

Large mounds of earth were evidence that the inhabitants of the islands had disposed of the remains of the zombies, and the more unfortunate few who'd been their prey.

Her hand shook, but in the distance, she spied hastily erected towers. "Makes sense," she whispered, pleased the babies remained asleep.

It wouldn't last long if the tingling in her breasts was anything to go by. They'd slept well for the last three hours, but they were only two months old and feed time was quickly coming upon her.

She needed to get across to the island before they woke and demanded her attention.

Her fingers gripped the wheel, eyes darting left to right as she slowed and steered over toward the bridge. The sign proclaiming 'Harbor Island Estate, 5km ahead' was bent and covered with brown... *Is that dirt?*

Blood. Old, dried blood spatter. The knowledge crashed into her mind, and she gulped as nausea rose in her belly, greasy and sour.

Once the vehicle stopped, she waited, wondering if someone would come out to greet her. The chains wound multiple times around the enormous gates, and she noted the large padlock. The gates themselves were topped with what appeared to be wickedly sharp barbed-wire and again the knowledge that she was now unprotected in no-man's-land with two tiny babies cut through her.

I should have stayed at the hospital. At least we were safe there.

The refrain she'd been fighting off looped through her mind. But she hadn't been able to stay, not really, or at least not long term. The guy in charge had made that clear. She wasn't a cook or a cleaner. Neither was she a doctor or nurse, and with no idea how to shoot, she'd been a liability. One day soon, they'd expect her to take up arms. The idea of that had her stomach sinking again.

Even now, looking around for any sign of the horribly mangled gray shufflers was more about staying safe than getting rid of them. The private religious school she'd attended had driven home the 'thou shalt not kill' too well, she mused.

A clanking sound echoed, and she turned back to the bridge. "Hey, you want in?"

"Yes," she called, feeling suddenly lightheaded.

"Move the car out of the way then, grab your stuff and—"

"I… I can't! I've got babies in the car. All their things."

The man sliding through the reinforced metal archway stared. "Babies?"

Her stomach knotted. "Twins. Two months. I can't carry all their stuff."

The man on the other side of the gate stared. "Damn it." He screwed up his face, as if thinking rapidly. "Alright then. I'll open the gate and you'll have to squeeze the car through. Once you're all inside, I'll radio across to let them know a car is coming."

Adrienne started the engine. The first baby woke and whimpered. "It's okay, sweetie. Mummy's here and I'll feed you soon." Of course, it wasn't like there was time to stop now, and she knew soon that whimper would become a cry. Wake the other twin, and the cacophony would begin.

The man opened the gate and the many locks hanging off it rattled loudly. She slid to a stop once she'd cleared the metal, and he closed it with a clang.

Turning off the engine, she slid from the car, aware that Fiona was now awake alongside Leanne and demanding her attention.

The man blinked again. "I need to radio ahead, as we aren't allowing cars on the bridge. They're getting ready to drop it."

"What?" Adrienne couldn't contain the squeak. "That means..." She must have looked like a gasping fish, mouth wide open.

"Not today, I mean. But in a few days. Planning. It's why they want no more cars coming this way. Don't want anyone to get caught up." He held up a handheld radio and began talking while advancing as the wails of the babies grew louder.

"Hush, my darlings," she whispered, opening the doors.

Even as she did, a dirge of moaning horror began, and the man looked to the gates. "You go. I'll let the other side know why. Now get those babies out of here, they're like bloody beacons to the undead."

He didn't have to tell Adrienne again. Slamming the door shut, she scurried around and hopped into the driver's seat. "Thanks!" She started the ignition and rolled the car forward. It wasn't until she'd travelled some distance that she finally settled, and once she'd safely cleared the bridge, a waiting committee had gathered.

⚜

*J*ack didn't know why he was here. The rotund little Mayor had insisted on his presence, along with a nurse and one administrator——a woman in her fifth decade. "I'm an Engineer," he growled.

"Yes, yes." The mayor's head bobbed up and down like a puppet working overtime. "Even so, you are the most senior surviving member of the council staff. The Executive is dead."

In the distance, he could see the little car moving slowly across the bridge, as if the driver was concerned about speed limits. The garbled message from Lucas was a woman with kids in the car... The zombies heard the grizzling and had converged en masse. But he had it under control. The cracks of shots echoed over the water. So here he was, a welcoming committee along with the mayor and a nurse.

When the car was within hearing distance, on a section of the bridge still some distance away, a sound—squalling, his mind told him—made itself heard. Now he could make sense of the message as the wails of infants in distress reached his hearing. "Shit! Baby."

The nurse—Sheila — a woman in her mid-thirties, grinned. "Babies," she corrected Jack.

He spun to stare at her. "What?"

"Multiples. That wail is more than one. And hungry. No wonder it attracted them. Even a whimper from an infant would do it. They're attracted to the sound, and I guess it's evolutionary." She glanced up the road, spying a shady park. "We need her to pull up over there. That sounds like hunger to me." Then she marched in that direction, and Jack rolled his eyes this time.

"Like, I'm a parking inspector?"

The mayor hee-hawed like a braying ass. "That's so funny, Jack. Yes, well, perhaps the formal welcome would be better coming from you." On that note, the little man scurried away, dragging the vacuous administration officer after him.

"And where do I house...?"

But if the mayor heard, well, he gave no sign. Neither did the woman with the fake black hair almost hidden beneath a bright orange emergency services cap, her pants a headache inducing lime green along with her turquoise y-neck tee.

Jack stomped up as the car came to a stop with a jerk. The woman behind the wheel, face stark white and drawn, stared at him. "I was told..."

The angry screams from the back of the vehicle had him peering inside the car. "Oh my god, new babies."

"Look, they're hungry and I need somewhere..."

His wits gathered. He pointed to the tree where the nurse waved. "Park in the shade and we can talk while you feed them."

The woman bit her lip and maneuvered to the spot indicated. As she climbed out, he didn't miss twin wet spots on her shirt. His mind whizzed on autopilot.

She grabbed a folding chair and set it up before grabbing first one then the other baby, which she deposited in the nurse's waiting arms.

"Oh dear, you're leaking," the woman murmured, and the driver glanced down at her shirt, before blushing a deep crimson. "Settle yourself and I'll change the first while you get started. Do you tandem feed?"

The woman blinked and nodded. "Normally, but I don't think..."

"That's okay, get yourself ready," soothed the nurse.

Before his surprised gaze, the young woman was unbuttoning her shirt, and he wondered if he'd entered the twilight zone.

With no concerns, she tugged on her bra, exposing a creamy breast interlaced with dark blue veins. The nipple rosy and distended. When the nurse handed the first baby over, it rooted for and found the nub, opened wide and took it within its mouth. The wailing slowed then as the nurse fished around in a large bag and settled to attend to the baby she still held.

Jack couldn't believe what he was seeing, neither could he look away. The woman, totally unconcerned now, cooed over the suckling child.

"Well, it seems like your feeding is established," Sheila commented, and this time, when the mother looked up, she clearly noted Jack staring.

"Oh... Sorry, you had questions."

Jack startled. "Oh, uh yes. My name's Jack... But maybe you'd like me to wait until you're done there?" He waved a hand at the baby.

"Fiona. She's older by fifteen minutes and always the first to make her presence known." With a smile, she nodded to the now quieter babe being rocked by the nurse. "That's Leanne. She's quieter, but already quicker to grasp onto what's happening. Look, I don't know the protocol here, but I came because I was told you're establishing an island for those who cannot fight. I need to be somewhere I can raise my babies. Somewhere safe. The hospital I left this morning..."

She gulped. "I have to be prepared to fight if I'm there. I can't. It's not what or who I am."

"And do you have a name?" Jack asked, noting that she swallowed.

"Adrienne Goolem. I'm a single mum. My husband, Darcy, died in the first wave. Because of my advanced pregnancy, I'd been sent to the hospital to wait out delivery and the all-clear. Except it didn't come."

Jack considered what she'd just shared. A widow. A young one at that. With twin girls. Soft, with a cloud of russet hair and bright blue eyes.

"Okay. I'm not the one who's in charge. That's the mayor—or self-styled, if you will. He sent me over to greet you but didn't make any arrangements for where you'll stay, and it'll be night soon."

She nodded, the baby releasing her breast, and she hefted it over her shoulder, rubbing until a tiny belch erupted and handed that baby to him. In his hands it felt... breakable. Fragile.

She adjusted her bra before exposing the other breast, accepting the second infant, then the nurse retrieved from his meaty hands. Fiona, he reminded himself again.

The feeding continued, and she cooed at the baby in her arms.

In his mind, Jack turned over the possibilities of where she'd stay while the nurse asked some questions he didn't really understand. Postpartum, vaccinations and testing, which the beauty, Adrienne, answered quietly.

The nurse placed the baby into the carrier after a nappy change, and as soon as Adrienne finished, she did the same with Leanne. Meanwhile, once the small folding chair was stashed, she raised herself up. Stared at him. "Where do I need to go? Do I need to find someone?"

"No. It's too late to be travelling far. I've got a beach house close to here, so come home with me." Truthfully, he did not know where that had even come from, just that on some level, it made sense.

"But the babies..."

He shrugged. "I'm not much of a sleeper anyway, and you'll be safer this way. Otherwise, we'd have to go to the police station, arrange accommodation and so on. We can sort all of that out tomorrow or the day after. When you're all rested, and I've had time to check in."

The nurse smiled. "Well, looks like everything is sorted for now. Given today's Saturday, there won't be anyone easy to contact tomorrow. Come down Monday if you can, get Jack here to bring you down to the clinic, so I can grab the babies' records and some of your details."

She retreated, and Jack watched her wander off to her car.

"Should I follow you?"

Jack shook his head. "No. I only live down the road, so I walked. If you're okay, I'll drive us there and we can get you settled."

*S*he didn't know who the man Jack was. He seemed nice enough, except for staring at her while she'd been feeding the babies. Not that unusual, she told herself. Before having babies, she'd also found the act both interesting and intimate.

"Umm, so why not put me up in a hotel?"

He quirked a brow. "Electricity and water. We're planning to move people from the further flung areas into the apartment blocks and houses, so we can keep used infrastructure to a minimum. So, currently, the buildings are full of workmen and people wandering in and out. Until I can get to my office on Monday, I can't say which buildings and apartments are available. And I'm guessing with the two in the back, you won't want lots of noise waking them during sleep time?"

The thoughtfulness threatened to undo her. "I'm... Gee, it's been a long time since anyone asked me what suited. I mean, the hospital was great. Safe. But there were rules, and I knew, soon enough, I'd need to fight..." Tears pricked her eyes. "It's why I left. I'd heard about the farms down south and nearly went there, but it was a long way and I'd have to travel by myself. With the babies. The stuff I heard."

She shuddered. "I couldn't take the risk, so instead when I heard about here, I made plans."

"It takes bravery to do something like that. But we're making plans too. Going to drop sections of the bridge so we only have to monitor the beaches. We can protect ourselves, and the island is big enough we can be self-sufficient. There're cattle being trucked in next week from the farms in the hinterland. We're getting paddocks ready…"

Her eyes widened, taking in the plans he was describing. "Wow. So, you think this shouldn't be an issue? Me and the babies staying?"

Jack turned, and the burn of his sapphire blue eyes shot right through her. "No. We've laid in supplies already and we've only got a few thousand people here. But the flip side is there isn't enough to look after everything all the time. If we play it clever, we can work on keeping the main lines for water, sewerage and so on in good repair so those living here have a decent standard of life."

Adrienne blinked. "That makes sense, but you've clearly done a lot in a few short months."

His generous mouth flattened. "We had to. Once people started dying and turning, there wasn't much else we could do. We have to keep everyone else well and healthy."

Considering his words, she could see the truth in them. But, given all that, it obviously couldn't be easy for anyone.

"Lots died here?"

"Yeah." Adrienne wondered if he realised how much that single word revealed.

He made one last turn then stopped in front of a high fence. Before she could hop out, he'd opened the gates and was back in the vehicle. They drove in and he parked the car in the yard.

Taking a moment to scan the house, she breathed deeply. It was a large, old-fashioned colonial structure. The high veranda sweeping around, freshly painted, the ornate fretwork the kind you saw on the grand old ladies of Brisbane. The ones where the rich lived.

"It's beautiful," she whispered.

"It was my parents' home. Now it's mine."

Once more, his tone revealed pain. She wondered if they'd been casualties of the plague that swept the nation, but kept her mouth shut. If he wanted to tell her, he would.

"Let's get you and the babies inside, then I'll ferry your stuff."

Jack reached down and gathered the nappy bags, leaving her to release the catches on the babies' seats, which also doubled as capsules.

He opened the door for her, and she stepped through the gate at the bottom of the steps, then shadowed him up. On the verandah, she turned and gasped, noting the view. The sea, now a dense blue-green, appeared to stretch forever and in the distance, and the bridge was illuminated by lights. "That's so pretty!"

"It's a bloody beacon, but until we can demolish part of it, we have to be on our guard." His words were terse.

She whipped around, almost dropping one baby carrier as she digested his words. "What do you mean?"

"As far as we can tell, zombies have terrible sight, though they aren't blind. They're attracted to sound and brightness. Smells as well. The babies are a huge beacon. But the lighting out there? It calls to them too. They mass and attack in bigger numbers when the lights comes on, wanting to get across to the island. They see the street lighting, and sometimes the sounds of people carry on really still days. It's why we fortified that section at the start of the bridge. It's also why we don't actually let cars on... especially at night. The sound travels and of course, newer models have automatic lights."

"Are we safe?" Nausea churned deep in her belly.

"At the moment, we appear to be. We think we've tracked down all the walkers on the island, though being sure is an entirely different thing. Some hide... It's like they've got better brain capacity than others. But the bridge... Until we sort it out, there's always going to be danger."

Have I left relative safety for something else? For less security in my stubbornness? For a moment, blind panic coursed.

He must have seen it on her face. He reached out, took the capsules from her grip and steered her toward a deep chair.

"We're safe in here. Now sit down and I'll get you a drink. Coffee? Tea? Water?"

"Water's... Water would be great thanks." Her gaze settled on Fiona and Leanne, and she exhaled. Working hard to get a grip on herself. "I'm sorry. I—"

He returned and squatted down beside her, handing over the cool glass. "It's okay. Really. This whole situation is... It sucks."

"Yeah. It really does."

"Just take a moment," Jack offered, "then I'll show you to the bedroom. Okay?" He disappeared for a moment before returning with a large glass in his hand.

She nodded. "Thanks. I'm... This is really kind. I mean, you don't even know my name." She thrust out a hand. "I'm Adrienne. My friends all call me Addie. These are my daughters, Fiona and Leanne." Addie pointed to the capsules.

He gazed at her, the look determined. "Welcome to my home, Addie. My parents..." now Jack shook his head. "My parents left the house to me, when they passed. It's big and empty and it's nice to have someone else in it."

She bit her lip. "Did they pass recently?"

A shadow crossed over his gaze. "Yeah. They were victims of the water plague."

"I'm so sorry. That would have been hard."

"It... It was."

She didn't miss the guilt that swept his features, and she knew, in that instant, he'd done what was necessary to give them peace. She reached out, gripped his icy hand. "You can't have had it easy."

He smiled. "No. Well, drink up. I'll go get the rest of your stuff." He pushed up and retreated, leaving her sitting there contemplating the mess they were all in.

CHAPTER 2

*J*ack couldn't say why he'd asked Adrienne to stay. Oh, he might, at a stretch, claim that it was the hour of the evening that she arrived. It could be the difficulty in raising someone to find her a secure location. They were all true. Up to a point.

It not the only reason. His mind niggled.

It was her.

The reason indefinable, but a feeling he couldn't ignore.

Jack considered himself a simple man with simple needs.

A home, safety. Warmth in the winter, cool in the summer. Three meals. Tasks that were meaningful.

So why this one woman, with two infants in tow?

He pushed the problem aside to consider later and began bringing up bags and boxes she'd stuffed into the boot of her car.

"How did you fit so much in there?" he called.

She blinked and took the box he held out to her at the top of the step.

"I didn't. The orderlies repacked everything so it would fit. Said the midwives and the doctors had insisted I had enough to make do."

She flipped open a box, and he saw a space age contraption with round plastic cups and bags, then blinked.

Addie blushed a deep rosy, red, and quickly closed it up before she moved to another box. She pulled out a large mat and a dismantled gym. "If you don't mind, I can put this on the floor, so they get some tummy time. The nurse told me it's important for their development."

"Uh sure. How about over here?" He pointed to a small area, and she nodded.

The next trip he brought up a long bag. "This?"

"It's a porta cot. Can we set it up in the bedroom? Then I can settle them in for the night?"

He nodded and led the way to his parents' room. It was large enough that he could set up the cot at the end of the heavy wooden bed they'd used their entire married life. He'd avoided the room except to find the keys to the safe, hidden in a bedside drawer.

"This is lovely," Addie said and turned a circle. "Are you sure?"

It should have felt wrong, but... "No, stay in here. There's an en-suite they had added fifteen years ago through here." He showed her a hidden door. "When Dad was diagnosed with cancer, they needed to have easy access. So, we enclosed a bedroom, added a dressing room and had the en-suite installed. I have my bathroom, down the corridor." He waved to the room on the other side of the hall.

She smiled tremulously, as if overwhelmed by his actions. Tears clung to her eyelashes, and it was like something lodged in his throat.

"I'll set up the cot, and you get the babies and anything you need in here. Then we'll organize some dinner."

He settled the bag on the bed and unzipped it, pulling out a mass of metal and blue padded material.

She ferried a small bag, two boxes of items and the mysterious space-age contraption, before carrying the babies up and with care lifted them from their travel cocoons.

He sighed. "How do you figure this stuff out?"

Addie laughed. "Let me. They made sure I knew how to erect and break it down." She moved with a grace he'd seen few exhibit, her actions sure, and finally she stood back. "There. Now let's just get the bedding in place."

Together they made up the bedding, and he watched as she kissed first one, then the other infant, and popped them into the bed. From a bag, she pulled a tiny white unit and sat it on the dressing table. "I'll hear if they fuss," she whispered and followed him from the room to the kitchen.

That night, Addie was lying in the enormous bed, wondering about how her life had changed. Darcy had been a good guy, not just because he was the biological father of Leanne and Fiona, but because he'd been responsible. The minute he'd known of her pregnancy, he'd insisted on marriage. He'd made plans for their future, cared for her in the early months during the miserable bouts of morning sickness. She'd felt cosseted and cared for.

They'd barely signed the paperwork for their marriage, and she'd been five months pregnant when their world changed.

They'd been driving home from the shops, the car full of baby clothes and groceries, when the radio station interrupted her favourite song.

"We interrupt this song with an urgent warning. A virus is sweeping Brisbane. Virulent and is believed to be water borne. Symptoms include: high fever, rapid heartbeat and quick onset of death. Doctors are investigating antibiotic treatment, but sources tell us, at this point, nothing is stemming the tide of the sickness."

Addie glanced at Darcy, noting the way his brown eyes widened. "Oh shit!" His face formed a dark frown.

Addie glanced at him; aware he'd been unwell most of the day. "Darcy?" The cough he exhibited only started in the last hour.

Panic filled his face. "What if...?"

She smiled and reached for him, but his skin was like fire. "Darc?" Addie dragged her hand back, curling her fingers.

"I've got the symptoms. Jeez, Addie. What if I've caught this? What if you get it?"

Addie slid a hand over her belly, feeling the first flutters within. "I... I'm sure we're fine. It's a flu you've caught, not this virus." But the fear in his voice tore at her guts.

Darcy wasn't satisfied. "I'll drop you at home and see if I can get an emergency appointment with the doctor."

He'd done just that. It was the last time Addie had seen him alive. Dr Vanderkeep had rung to let Addie know they had admitted Darcy to the hospital and the prognosis grim. "Addie, he's got all the symptoms and in the last hour, he's dropped into a coma."

"Should I...?"

"No Addie. You're at risk, with the pregnancy. Stay as far away as you can. Remain at home but call me if you show any symptoms. We don't know if this can also be transmitted via the air. You could already be infected, or you could be immune. We just don't know."

"I... Ok, Dr Vanderkeep. I'll stay home, just keep me updated, okay?"

Three days later, the call had come that Darcy had passed.

She'd stayed home. The funeral home she'd contacted, overwhelmed, they'd said that they'd collect his body a few days after Darcy's death. Even now, she didn't know if they had, because the explosion of madness had taken place, or where he'd been buried.

That was a few months ago. She'd given birth naturally at term to the girls, and they'd kept her at the birthing center in the hospital, because there wasn't a lot of call for use afterwards. With no secure home to return to, and no assistance, it had been too dangerous to do anything else. There'd been a few other women in her situation, but slowly they'd either left the center or accepted the new reality.

Darkness enveloped the earth as Addie rose from the bed and moved to the verandah, the French windows open to admit the cool beach breeze.

She wondered if Jack was awake, also thinking about how his life had changed.

Jack.

She already knew he was a good man.

She bit her lip. "No one needs to know about your crushes, Addie. Remember, that's how you and Darcy ended up as parents." Except he hadn't lived to see his girls.

He hadn't lived long enough to regret their hasty decisions.

She twisted the gold band on her finger.

Without Darcy, she had responsibilities she couldn't share with others. A life to live. Decisions to make.

She just wondered, if somewhere out there, the shell of the man who'd fathered her children still walked.

*J*ack heard the movement on the verandah. Reaching into the drawer beside the bed, he tugged out the tiny pistol he'd carried with him for the last six months.

It was protection, but he hated the necessity for it. And now with a woman and two infants in the house... He moved, silently he hoped, clad in only the pajama bottoms he'd fished out for while Adrienne and the babies were in residence.

He'd stepped around, just enough to catch sight of her, clutching the railing, the fitful moonlight limning her body.

Lush, with firm full breasts. Fertile with round hips. Her hair billowing around her shoulders. She'd caught her hair up with a clip, but now he could see the true splendor of it.

His body firmed. He moved, adjusting his pants. *She's a nursing mum, you dickhead.*

It didn't help though, because for the first time in a long while, he experienced interest in a woman.

His mind cast back, trying to work out when last he'd had those kinds of thoughts, and to his surprise it was well over a year since he'd broken up with Sarah and come back home. A year and a couple of months. He couldn't even remember the month, and that surprised him.

Since then, he'd licked his wounds, discovering she'd been busy with another man while he'd been working hard, climbing the ladder. Building his career so he could afford a suitable house, a lifestyle she'd appreciate.

Then came the zombies. His parents. . . Now he shied away from remembering. He stepped closer. "Everything okay?"

Addie turned. "Oh, you're awake." He didn't miss the flick of her eyes, the way they travelled down his chest then moved to the view. "Yeah. I just... Lots happened in the last year or so. It's hard to imagine back... To think that this time last year, Darcy and I were just starting out. I wasn't even pregnant."

"Darcy, was your husband?" He nodded to the ring she was still twisting on her fingers.

"Yeah. We'd been dating for a couple of months, nothing too serious. He was a plumber, and I was the girl from the coffee shop and carvery. Made him coffee every day when he and his workmates came in for lunch. One day, he slipped a card into my hand when he paid. He'd written on the back, 'You're cute and we should date.'" Addie laughed.

It warmed him that she'd experienced fun. But he knew—or at least guessed—that Darcy had passed. "What happened?"

"He came home one day. Didn't feel so flash, and we both decided if he woke up feeling crappy the next day, he needed to rest. Darcy had been working around the clock on a commercial building in Brisbane. He took the day off, and he got worse while we were out, getting stuff for the babies. I insisted he go to the doctors after the announcement on the news. He..." She hiccupped. "Darcy didn't come home."

Jack reached out for her hand, after noticing it shook. "You were okay?"

Addie shrugged. "Darcy bought a little house on the edge of town. We'd begun to set up the nursery because we knew they were twins. The ultrasound gave it away." She laughed again, but now there was a watery sound. "I made do until I went into labor. I got myself to the hospital, and they kept me there. Said it was for our safety. They were probably right. But the thing is, I have no mementos. No photos. Nothing to remember my past life with. Nothing to give them when they get older."

His mind blanked. He had his home, photos, family recordings. "You want some of them?" For a second, urgency drove him, made him want to take the chance to give her what she'd lost. He snapped back to reality. *It wasn't safe. May never be again.*

She shrugged. "It's not like I can go back, is it? I'm nearly two hundred kilometers away. And with the babies...?" She sighed, and he knew she was aware of the dangers. "I don't even know what's left. They said at the hospital there'd been widespread looting. People looking for stuff so they can survive."

He waited because what else was there to say? I'm sorry, didn't even touch the sides of the grief she must feel.

"Look, even thinking about that makes me sound shallow. I'm not, and I want to help. I want to be useful." She gripped his hands, as if willing him to understand and accept her words.

"You will be. Right now, your focus is those babies."

Addie sniffed. "At the hospital, they wanted me to do stuff that wasn't..." She tugged her hand free.

He felt the loss of the warmth that she exuded. It took immense concentration to ignore the pull of her.

She dragged her hand through the disarrayed red tresses. "They were pretty clear. The administrators said we all had to be useful. I would put the babies in the creche, and I could either join a gathering party to collect food and things from the locality or I needed to train as a guard. Stupidly, I actually thought a guard would be okay, so I spent a day..." Pain dripped in her voice now.

"Did they kill zombies?"

She nodded. "Three kids. I couldn't... I threw up. On the roof and some of them, from the looks they gave me? They knew I couldn't do that. It's when I decided I had to get away. I'd heard of you guys. That you were on an island and there was a chance of safety and a normal life. I had to take it. You know? For me and for them."

Jack understood and stepped up, took her hand, and tugged her into his arms. Held her close, hoping he could for a moment give her peace of mind.

His body, though, wanted to betray him as the scent of her rose in his nostrils. Roses, he thought and closed his eyes, willing everything to loosen up a little.

"God! You're a good listener," she muttered and pulled away. "Maybe we could be friends?"

Now, Jack gave a nod, not yet willing to chance his voice giving away the emotions churning inside him. For now, the concept of 'friends' was a mere dip in the well of what he wanted.

She smiled. "I should head back to bed. They'll be waking again soon, knowing my luck. Looking to feed."

"Yeah. Okay."

She stepped away, and he waited for a moment before retreating to his own empty bed.

He lay awake for a long time. Listening and trying to sort out the jumble in his mind. Because he didn't just want to be friends. He wanted more. Lots more. That it was so unlike his usual careful way with women confused him. Frustrated him.

On a growl he finally turned over, thwacked his pillow with a balled fist and waited for sleep to claim him.

CHAPTER 3

*A*ddie woke early, the girls having slept six hours. She took time showering and dressing in fresh underwear, and was just about to pull on jeans when Fiona fussed.

Picking her up, Addie quickly changed the baby and settled onto the bed to feed her when Leanne woke. She might be the quieter but when her belly was empty, she could get up a wail. Popping Fiona down, she scooted over, picked up the twin and set about changing her too.

With quick moves, she shuffled pillows around and settled both the babies to feed. It had taken a little while to get the routine down pat, but now she could do it alone, and that brought a sense of achievement.

She was just finishing up when the sound of movement in the house caught her attention.

Jack. He was a good-looking man. Tall—at least six foot three, with an angel's face, with chiseled high cheekbones. Piercing blue eyes and a hint of golden stubble edging along his jawline.

She knew he was muscular... That had been clear last night when he'd joined her on the verandah. His chest carried a sprinkling of hair. Not too much, but enough to tangle her fingers in.

She caught herself. "What on earth are you thinking, Addie? He wouldn't be interested in you. You've got the babies to consider and…" She ran her hand over her face. No, now was definitely not the time for lustful thoughts.

With both twins happy, she slid them onto the bed and rose, sliding into jeans and a t-shirt, then picked them both up and over her shoulder, she headed into the lounge.

Jack was busy in the kitchen. Had he heard her? He surprised her as she was rising from placing the babies on the mat. He extended the mug in his hand. "Coffee?" then his face screwed up. "Are you allowed with them?"

She laughed. "Absolutely. I just have to keep the number of cups down, but that's pretty simple as I usually drink lots of water."

She followed him into the kitchen. It was a cottage style affair with whitewashed cabinets, a new large freestanding gas oven. The most amazing thing of all was that every surface was spotless. "Do you have a cleaning lady?"

He laughed. "I wish. No. Mum taught me when I was young that a clean kitchen means less work. I guess those teachings just stuck."

His confident movements were hypnotic.

"I got some breakfast going. Hope you like eggs? I guessed you probably need to eat well."

"I do, thanks. Look, you've been really kind. I appreciate this, but you don't have to wait on me. Honestly, I want to pull my weight in the community."

He turned. "I know. But I guess, it's nice having someone else here. It's a big house and I putter around."

"Will you tell me what happened?"

He knew what she meant with her quiet words. The understanding was there in his gaze, but he didn't answer the question.

They worked quietly and soon he had scrambled eggs and toast ready along with aromatic coffee in heavy round mugs.

Afterwards, they moved to the lounge so she could watch the babies and eat, and settled at the coffee table and she waited for him to explain.

He lifted the fork, sighed, and placed it at the edge of his plate. "When the plague hit, we were reasonably safe. Mum and Dad had a supply of bottled water. I'd spoken with the guy treating the water and he thought that using the new disinfection protocol... using chlorine would kill any virus existing in the water. I didn't know then, but it didn't. Or at least not immediately. It was two weeks after, when the supply of bottle water ran out. I suggested using the tanks, but mum laughed. She used that as our fallback system, during dry times for the gardens."

Addie's gut curled. She was pretty sure she knew what came next. "And?"

"The old, the ill and those with a predisposition, according to our doctor, were the first to get sick. Mum held in there, when Dad got ill. It was quick. Only three days from when he caught it to when he... succumbed."

"You had to..." She couldn't say the words as the sickness congealed in her belly, the eggs now sitting precariously.

"Yeah. Mum just seemed to go within a day after that. I got them both to the doctors. He told me to leave it to them, but I couldn't." His eyes shone with tears and Addie reached out, took his hand and squeezed. "I looked them in the eyes. Then I pulled the trigger."

He was stronger than her. She couldn't even shoot at strangers, let alone parents.

"What kind of unfeeling creature am I?" The garbled words carried so much self-loathing, and for a moment she wondered just how much that had scarred him.

"No, Jack. You did what you had to do. What... Where did you bury them?" She wasn't sure she'd be comfortable with the knowledge they were buried in the backyard. That would be hard to take, even for the next twenty-four hours she was to stay here.

"The doc had our guys dig big pits; said the only thing to do was to mass cremate. We delivered the bodies. They'd been running pretty much twenty-four hours a day. There were thousands, Addie. Can I call you that?" Now he reminded her of a little boy. Lost and alone.

Unable to contain herself, she reached over and cupped his cheek. "You can. You're my friend." She meant it, and she'd be damned if she'd hurt him with her own urges.

"For weeks the smell and smoke were awful. Mum and Dad were among the last. We covered the remains with soil and those left... We made do. Doc, until he got sick, the Mayor and I, are working with what's left of the police. The hospital is bare bones, but we're keeping it open. Keeping the water flowing, the lights on. We'll survive."

If he had anything to do with it, they'd do more than just survive, Addie thought. "What kind of communication do you have with the mainland?"

He laughed, the sound rough. "Phones went out, but not before we got news of why this happened."

She jerked. "What do you mean?"

"Someone tampered with the water supplies. I heard it was supposed to be an inoculation that went wrong. A mutation of a virus introduced caused the zombies. The chlorine did eventually work, but not soon enough to keep most of the populace from falling ill. Those that survived the initial wave, caught the illness from bites. It's why we have to cut ourselves off. Stop any of the zombies from making it to the Island."

She had heard nothing of this. But then that was six months ago and two of them she'd spent holed up in the hospital at the edge of Brisbane. And in her grief, she'd not listened to the news, focusing instead of surviving and growing the babies who'd rested in her womb.

"So, what now?"

"I'm trying to find a way to cut us off. We need to take out the bridge or even just a bit. Enough that they can't get across. We've got some amateur radio operators and reckon if we can find others we can still communicate. We can get across to the mainland in boats. There's more than enough here."

Addie considered his words and opened her mouth when a rapid knocking came from the verandah. His brow creased, and he rose. "Back in a moment."

She didn't miss the way his hand moved to the small holster she'd seen at his hip.

Shadowing him as far as the door, she watched the frown on his brow deepen. "What's up, Tom?"

"One of the buildings... We missed a zombie or more than one and they've breached it. We got problems."

Her gut clenched hard.

"I... Just a moment." He appeared at the top of the steps. "I have to go. I'm needed. You need to lock the doors. Stay inside. I'll be back as soon as I can."

***

*J*ack hurried down the steps, following Tom. At the gate to the steps, he stilled and looked up.

Addie had wandered out, her face pale and strained. "I'll lock up. Go inside. Keep the babies safe."

Tom's look was quizzical. "Babies? Something I don't know?"

Jack shook his head. "Addie arrived yesterday with her twins. Little girls. She's staying with me until..." He couldn't say until there was somewhere else, because this new problem reinforced that nowhere was really safe. Not until they'd hunted down every fucking zombie and eradicated it. Until the bridge was demolished. Until they could be sure.

"A woman with babies. Staying with you? Are you mad? Stinky nappies and crying babies. I wouldn't have taken you for that."

Sarah hadn't either, not that she'd wanted kids, or *'squalling brats who'll ruin my figure'* she'd said. No. She'd wanted the lifestyle. A show house. The social engagements. Most of all, she'd craved the connection to his family and their comfortable financial position.

He needed to get his head in the game, though. "What happened?"

"Last night, a zombie we obviously missed during the rounding up got into the waterfront hotel."

The building they'd been refurbishing, earmarked to house families. They'd remodeled the structure with large three—and four—bedroom apartments, located only three blocks from the school. With the grounds reworked and a renewed with playground equipment, it made a perfect hub for younger members of the island's survivors.

"And?" he nudged.

"The workmen there got out, but the staff didn't. We lost fifteen that we know of. The crew contained a 'new-turn', but the original is still out there. Spoke with the Sarge and he wants us to comb the area near the marina. Thinks he might be hiding."

He'd known Thomas for most of his life, and when he'd returned a fully-fledged police officer, it felt like he hadn't really changed. Except he took the motto of With Honor We Serve seriously. Even though he'd had the chance to walk away from the force, and join the newly elected council, he'd refused.

"The state of the building?"

Thomas' face was gray. "Bad. Terrible. Not sure anyone would want to move into it now. Holes in the walls, bits of bodies strewn all over the place. Glass smashed. Might be better to demolish, honestly."

Jack wanted to ask Thomas to swing by, but he understood time was of the essence. The zombies might prefer the night, but were just as dangerous in the day, when they could see better, according to the doc.

They drove quickly, but carefully, Thomas' gaze whipping from side to side, clearly scanning for a sign of where the zombie had gone.

At the marina, they stopped. Climbed from the car.

"It's three kilometers, Tom. You reckon he'd have come this far?"

Tom turned to look at him. "We don't know. We haven't established a ballpark on how fast they move, yet. There's been chatter that there's some that are brutal fast. Almost as if they've evolved, then there're the originals. The old walking dead style zombie driven by hunger who shuffle. And there's the other thing we don't know. Once they've fed, how long can they hide out? It's only been just over six months and we haven't amassed any real useful information about them. They don't think like we do, so profiling them it almost impossible." Frustration laced the words, and Jack could understand just how much Tom hated the not-knowing.

They searched for hours. The residents of the yachts and boats hadn't seen or heard anything. Neither had those holed up in the apartment buildings overlooking the marina. The sun was high in the sky by the time Tom drove him to the Waterfront Hotel.

At the entrance, he saw for himself the drunken hang of the doors. Cleaners had obviously been through cleaning up the remains, but spatters and unidentifiable masses still adorned the walls.

Many windows were smashed, and he sighed. "The building can be rehabilitated again, it's true, but we need to talk to the people. I can't and won't ask anyone to put in more time or to move in here knowing this happened."

He certainly wouldn't want Addie and the babies living here. It wasn't secure, and he had a sneaking suspicion she wouldn't want to live here, in the knowledge of so many violent deaths.

"I need to get to the office, see the mayor."

"Ahh, you won't get him. We tried to talk to him first, on the way to come get you. He was heading out sailing with his admin, Paula. Said the day was far too nice to waste." There was no missing the sarcasm lacing Thomas' words.

Jack turned away, surprise uppermost in his mind as the importance of the information sunk in. *Too nice a day...* "Fuck. Okay, we need to call a meeting, and talk to the people's representatives. Get their feedback." He hated when this happened, but the mayor didn't seem to think that the day-to-day nitty gritty work should be his responsibility. Jack didn't particularly like the man, and really despised having to pick up the slack, but it had to be done and his firm sense of responsibility wouldn't allow him to ignore what needed to be done.

"I'll tell the Sarge when I get back to the office. What about you?"

Jack considered. He needed to get into the office, look at the plans they'd already put in place, and see what alternatives they could employ if they abandoned the building. "I need to get home. Let Addie know. Grab something to eat, then head into the office."

Thomas smiled but it appeared forced, and Jack frowned. "What?"

"Sure, she's not more than just staying with you?" Thomas' words carried a bite.

Jack's protective instincts rose. "Tom, she's got infants. Arrived yesterday and she's frightened. Where was I going to send her?"

"Yep. Okay, if you say so." Thomas clearly didn't believe him though, and that bit.

"Look, just drop me off. I'll swing by later to see the Sergeant. Until then, keep it quiet."

"Whatever, man. Just think though, Sarah wouldn't have welcomed you home looking like that."

Glancing down, Jack understood exactly what Thomas was saying. Dirt, grass and something that was suspiciously blood-like streaked his clothes. "Damn." Maybe he could get inside, shower and change before Addie could catch sight of him.

He jumped from the car, let himself into the yard, and was halfway up the steps when Addie opened the door. "You're back. Good. Do you want..." Her words broke off. "Oh, my... Are you hurt? Bitten?" Her face took on a pallor, with wide eyes.

"No. I was looking, and we brushed through stuff. I'm okay." *Weirdly, he wanted to assure her they were safe. All of them.*

She sailed forward though, her hands framing his face. "You're sure?"

He nodded and held out his hands. "Absolutely. Just messy. I need to wash and change, then head into the office."

As if his words triggered something, Addie stepped back, nodded. "Of course. You should eat. I'll make sandwiches. Go shower."

He could get seriously used to this, he thought, retreating. It was nice to have someone to come home to.

*A*ddie had to contain the last vestiges of fright that fizzled through her veins. He'd looked tired and worn and the mess of his clothes. . . *Blood!* Of course, she'd thought he might be injured. "You reacted like an idiot," she told herself sternly. All over him like a rash and touchy-touchy. God, he must think her some needy woman.

She'd never been one before and refused to let the situation now turn her into some namby-pamby insecure princess.

Instead, she returned to the kitchen, pleased the babies were down for a nap while she rattled about. Cheese slices, fresh firm tomatoes and what looked suspiciously like cured ham would do the job. Being wholly unsure what he'd prefer, she laid all the items cut and ready to use on the table, theorizing that do-it-yourself would solve the issue of making something he couldn't eat or didn't like.

Next, she made a carafe of coffee, finding the filter papers and unmilled beans in the fridge. It had been a long while... Over eight months since she'd had a decent brew and the scent of fresh ground coffee was like ambrosia.

By the time he returned, she was sitting at the table waiting for him.

"Looks great. But you should have started."

Addie grinned. "No. I wanted to hear how you got on."

His frown was deep. "Bad. There's at least one loose zombie and we aren't sure if there are others. I have to go into the office, because I'll need to meet with the reps to see how they want to handle it."

"Handle catching the zombie?"

"No. The building. The staff were setting up when the zombie broke in. We lost fifteen, we think. The place is a mess."

She shivered. "I wouldn't want to live there. Not after what you've said."

Jack nodded, and she took a bite of the sandwich she'd put together. "Yeah. I reckon plenty of others would say that too. But we need to look at how we're going to accommodate those we had earmarked for the building."

"But... I mean, how are you working that out?"

He shrugged. "We offer families larger apartments. Singles in the hotels and—"

"Hang on. Families in larger units. Does that mean you're working out how many people there are in each family when you offer them a place?"

His food stilled on the way to his mouth, and he looked at her, surprise blooming on his features. "I... No."

"Why not?" She really wanted to know. Would they have offered her something with four bedrooms when she only really needed three? "So, a family of five could end up in a three-bedroom unit?"

"I... I guess." He took a bite, chewed and swallowed, while Addie watched. "Would that be a problem?"

She nearly snorted at that. "Yes. Sometimes it might be."

"I'm..." When he put his food back onto the plate and stared at her, she shook her head.

"You really don't have a clue, do you? Sometimes kids shouldn't share rooms. Especially if they don't get along, or have issues." Then she realised he might think she was lecturing him and closed her eyes. "I'm sorry, I shouldn't have said anything. You're doing the best you can, right?"

Jack reached out and took her hand. "I'm not upset, Addie. Actually, this is stuff we hadn't considered. I don't suppose..." Then it was his turn to stop. "No, you're busy with the babies." He pulled away, and she silently mourned the loss of the touch.

"No. Tell me."

"I was just thinking, we've been so busy trying to survive, this stuff totally passed us by. Would you be interested in helping me? I don't have the time and this... I mean these niceties don't always occur to me."

Warmth suffused her. A different kind, but no less seductive. He was asking for her assistance. "I'd have to bring the babies, but I'd really like to help." And she would. Rather than just sitting around and keeping house, she'd be useful. Useful in a way that didn't run contrary to her beliefs.

"Wow. Look, I have to go into the office this afternoon. I can either wait and we all go in, or I'll bring some stuff home for you."

The way he said home had her eyes pricking with tears. "I'd love to come. The babies are due to wake up soon. I can bring their mat and the bouncers. And it's not like I have bottles to warm up."

His face heated, and she understood that the talk of breastfeeding embarrassed him. Once again, she wanted to bite her lip because she spoke too much. "I'm sorry, I shouldn't..."

"No. I'm just not used to..." He cleared his throat. "Do what you need to and let me know when you're ready."

They finished lunch in silence, and when she rose, it was to the wail of a baby.

"I'll clear the table and wash up. Go. The babies need you."

His solicitousness was enough to have the tears welling up again.

$\mathcal{J}$ack washed up, letting his mind blank. Refusing to acknowledge that in the bedroom, she was feeding those babies. It wasn't easy because he was already so damned attracted to her, that the knowledge was more than a distraction. The earth mother aspect of the intimate task drew him.

Her quiet manner had him feeling more at home than he'd ever experienced with any other woman. To be honest, it was both scary and exciting by equal turn.

Her skin, when he'd touched her, was fine and soft. Not caked in makeup. Her lush body encased in regular clothing, not the latest fashion that bared almost everything, and it was more a case of what he couldn't see, that had his mind buzzing.

She had no airs and graces. Addie was just a kind woman who wanted to be useful and care for her children.

But did she want more? Was she even ready because her husband wasn't even dead a year?

On a growl, he headed into the study, needing to take his mind off the situation of Addie and what his body demanded. His textbooks filled the bookshelf, and he made himself consider the situation with the bridge. That was a priority. How could they demolish the sections he'd earmarked without causing more damage and the loss of lives?

He'd picked one off the shelf and had settled in, the book lay open on his lap as he scoured the index when he heard her. "Jack?"

"Done already?" He snapped the book shut, then internally cursed, wondering if he'd scared them.

"Yeah. Here, you take Fiona and I've got Leanne." She slid the waiting baby into his arms. It wasn't the first time he'd held one, but somehow there was more meaning in this exchange.

He looked down into the tiny face, noting the button nose and the waving arm that captured his finger.

"Hey there," he murmured.

"She likes you," Addie said, and he looked up to see the smile on her face. "We should get moving, I guess."

He hooked the two bouncers under his arm and let her lead the way, waiting only while she locked the door at his urging.

They settled the babies in the car. He'd had to watch Addie so he could see how the capsule secured around the infant. He was, nonetheless, pleased with himself once he completed the task.

The remote, he hadn't used the night before, in his pocket had the gates to the property opening, and he started the engine, then backed the car down the short driveway onto the road. Jack clicked the button again, waited for the gates to close, then drove off.

"You didn't use one of those last night," she queried.

"I left it at home, The pedestrian gate isn't on the system. I'll need to give you one of the remotes," he offered.

She turned. "But tomorrow…"

"I'd rather you stayed with me. With things as they are, and two tiny babies, I'd feel better."

"I can stand on my own two feet, you know."

He smiled a little at the terse comment. "I'm sure you can. To be honest, I'm being selfish. I need help at work. You need somewhere to stay. It's nice coming home to a house with people in it, and not just being on my own. And I'm finding I rather like those munchkins in the back."

Silence reigned. "Really?"

He didn't miss the skepticism in her voice. "Really. Please stay."

"I'll think about it," she murmured.

"Addie—"

"I can't take pity or charity, Jack."

He considered her words as he steered the car towards the building. "It's neither Addie. To be honest, you'd be helping me out. I don't enjoy living alone, something I've determined since my parent's death. The house needs noise and kids. I also suck at cooking, so if you're any good, that would help me out too. I've been living on toasted sandwiches forever." He laughed a little. "And the washing ends up on the line for a week, or more if I don't have time or inclination to bring it in."

Now, Addie sighed. "Well, maybe just until you need us to move out. I don't want to overstay my welcome."

It occurred to him, as he parked the car, that wasn't something Sarah would have ever said, or worried about. "Trust me, you'd know if I didn't want you there."

"Let's take it a week at a time, okay?" Now they moved with speed, him gathering Leanne and the bouncers, while Addie dealt with Fiona and the large bag she seemed to carry everywhere. He guessed it carried nappies and the like, not that he'd know for sure, not having that much experience.

They hastened with him shadowing her, ensuring her safety with the bulk of his body.

Inside, he hit the button on the car key to lock it, then followed suit with the building locks. "This way," he motioned her down a long corridor.

"Nice building," she muttered, head turning left and right.

"I guess." Jack shrugged. "There's only six of us now, using this set up. It was meant as a regional office. Beforehand, there were, I don't know, about thirty in the offices and library? Plus, outdoor staff."

"That's a lot to lose," she whispered and entered the office space

at the rear. The area was a mass of partitions, large drawer like cabinets and folders. He wondered what it was she saw. If she understood
any of the functions these items fulfilled. Probably not, he told
himself. Few did.

"Set the babies up here and I'll get you going with a computer
and see if I can find a badge." He settled the capsule he carried gently
on the floor and smiled at the baby.

"Badge?"

He glanced up. "Grants access to the buildings and systems. You'll
need it." He didn't miss the way her lips flattened. "It's necessary.
There are systems I can't override. I don't have anyone who knows
how to do that, anyway, so it's not like I can choose."

She nodded, though he wasn't sure that settled her concerns.

CHAPTER 4

Addie gazed at the screen. He'd given her a crash course in how to navigate the information, but though she'd trained in IT systems, none of it was as intricate as what she now saw.

"We're pretty sure there're others on the mainland who survived, but this backup is a remote echo of what existed at the time of the internet crash." He'd taken up position just behind her. Not for the first time, she was supremely aware of his proximity.

"What happened? I didn't hear any...?" She quieted, not having the words to describe the sudden cessation of the communications systems.

"We don't really know either. We just got up one morning and all the communications systems, telephone and internet were dead. It ranks up there with contamination of the water systems, and if I were a cynical person—which I'm not—I'd wonder if it was part of a greater plan."

She bit her lip and nodded. "That makes sense. I mean, a profound virus and no communications. Anyone could come in and take—"

"Control. I agree."

She waited in the silence, sure he'd say something more, but he rolled his chair back. "Familiarize yourself with the system, I need to check on this stuff from Thomas. I don't plan to be too long."

Then he was up and gone. Losing his presence was like taking off a blanket on a cold wintry day. She turned to gaze at her babies. "I'm going to have to watch myself." Relying on Jack might become more than a security blanket, her mind warned. Too bad that other, totally indefinable region of emotion told her. Already in too deep.

A burst of anger flared. This is what she'd done with Darcy. Dove in and later on, while she didn't regret her babies, she wished she'd waited on a different level. Taken the time to know Darcy before falling pregnant. The extra strain, knowing two tiny lives were on the way, had cooled the passion between them long before she'd expected. Not that they hadn't been thrilled with the news, but...in hindsight, she wasn't sure she could say they'd have stayed together.

Turning back to the computer, she opened a tab and began looking for the files he'd requested.

*J*ack watched her from his office. Knew something bothered her. Watched as she'd stop, flick the pencil in her hand as she was searching.

He shook his head and rose from his chair.

He needed to concentrate. They had to bring that section of the bridge down. He'd racked his memory, but they had taught him about erecting structures, not demolishing them. On his books shelf he had tomes named 'Principles of Engineering', 'Steel Concrete and Other Building Blocks' and even, 'Safeguarding What You've Built— A Primer for new Architects and Engineers'. There wasn't a title focusing on 'Demolishing Structures in case of a Zombie Apocalypse.' The whimsy of his thoughts made him smile.

"So, where do I even begin looking?" he murmured.

"What exactly are you looking for?"

Her question shocked him, and he jerked and turned. "Have you been standing there long?"

"Not really, no. But the babies will wake soon, and I wanted to let you know I'm going to run to the bathroom then grab a drink of water before they…"

"There's bottled water on the cooler. Use that, not the tap water, please."

She blinked as if processing the words. "Oh… Oh right! Yes, of course." Turning away she wandered off and not for the first time, he wondered about the woman who had appeared on the bridge yesterday with infants and a soft manner that intrigued him.

He heard the babies stirring and moved into the office where she'd laid them down.

Such little things, he mused. And yet, with only a day's acquaintance, they'd somehow come to represent hope to him. The possibility of a future he'd lost sight of. "I will do what's necessary to keep you safe. And your mother too."

He heard her shuffling about in the kitchen, so he unfastened the first baby, then the other than, having watched what she needed, he set out the change mat, wipes and fresh nappies for them. He guessed nursing and changing was a more involved matter with two and that she probably would benefit from assistance.

"Oh, thanks for that," she indicated to the way he'd prepared everything. "I don't have a way to feed them both at the same time and was wondering how I'd—"

"You're not alone, Addie. I'll help as best I can."

Her eyes widened. "I… Thank you." Her voice turned husky, as if overwhelmed by the offer.

"Hand me one of them. I'll change them and you can feed. I'll do my best to distract…" he squinted. "Fiona?"

She lifted the baby into his arms. "Wow. Most people can't tell them apart."

"She's got a rounder face, and more hair."

"She does. You know how to change…?"

"I'll muddle through," he assured her and turned to the mat, looking for the snaps he'd seen in the baby's crotch.

He didn't watch as Adrienne fed the baby. He felt she deserved her privacy. But his stomach tied in knots.

"It's okay," she murmured.

"Uh, what?"

"You can turn around, Jack."

His shoulders hunched involuntarily. "Uh, no. It wouldn't be right."

She sighed, and he guessed that summed up the strange situation they found themselves in. The more time he spent with Addie, the more time he wanted to spend with her. Getting to know her.

Like magic or quicksilver, his mind added.

He focused on the baby in his arms, wiggled his fingers over her face, before gently touching her button nose. Her legs thrashed, and she gurgled. "You're pretty cute, aren't you? Bet you think you've got it made. Dinner on…" his mind blanked for a second, "tap. Someone to clean your nappies. Yeah, you clever girl."

"That's pretty good, you know. Talking to them helps create a bond, the nurse told me. At this age, that's important." Addie's voice was closer now, and he steeled himself, but her hand touched his shoulder and he turned. Leanne was over her shoulder and Addie's clothes were back in position. "Leanne's finished, if you pass up Fiona, I'll feed her, and you might change this one?"

"Sure." He accepted the baby and as Addie leaned over him, he couldn't miss the unmistakable scent of luscious woman. His groin tightened.

It was only when she moved away, he could allow himself to breathe again, but the hint of her remained, wafting around him. With a sigh, he settled to change the nappy.

*A*ddie's emotions were still all over the place, but something about Jack soothed the ragged feelings that roiled inside herself. She loved her babies and wanted only the best for them. It was imperative to build a stable life for them, one that made her feel like part of a greater community.

As the baby finished feeding, she popped her over the shoulder and rubbed Fiona's back. Once the tiny belch erupted, she moved the baby into the crook of her arm and re-adjusted her clothing.

"What more did you want to achieve?" Addie enquired of Jack, and he turned now to look at her.

"Huh?"

"You were muttering in your office before. Is there something I can help with?"

He grimaced. "Not unless you know something about demolishing a bridge."

Addie bit her lip. "Can't you just blow it up?"

Jack rubbed his hand over his face, and she had to fight the need to soothe the concern he radiated. "We don't have explosives, and even if we did, there's no one here to lay them. I need to find another way."

"Oh." She could now understand his frustrations. No explosives meant finding another way to achieve the same outcome. She wracked her brains, considering memories of events that had occurred worldwide before they were cut off. "What about making your own? With fertilizer?"

"If there's fertilizer, it's going to be like gold. We're going to be clearing areas for farming. I doubt they could spare any. That's even if I knew the quantities that would be necessary to achieve the outcome."

The bubble of satisfaction that had grown within her, burst. "Sorry," she muttered.

"What for? You made a suggestion, and it had the possibility of being viable. If people don't make suggestions, we may not be able to work out how to fix our problems. And no one person will have all the answers."

She nodded, though it was slow because of her disappointment.

"We should head home. I've not found anything useful on the shelves and we've got you in the system."

Glancing in the library's direction, she called to Jack, "Could I perhaps borrow a book or two?"

He blinked. "Sure. Leave the babies with me. We've got time for you to browse."

She smiled at him, slid the capsule she had scooped up with Fiona inside, and popped it beside a chair at the doorway. Jack settled into the seat and popped the second capsule beside the first.

The room was large and had a distinctly musty smell. She didn't care though, because in the hospital, there'd been no access and since then... This was the first opportunity in months to read a book, and at least since Darcy had left. Her finger slid over the plastic covered titles. There were romance novels and gritty murder mysteries. On the shelf was the latest Suzi Love title. "I haven't read this one," she muttered and kept scanning the shelves for something else once she'd slid it under her arm.

At the end of the row, she peeked over to where Jack was playing with the children and sighed. He's so good with them. She forced herself to continue prowling the shelves and picked up another book by a well-known Australian author. "I'll have this one too."

Now she headed for the non-fiction titles via the baby books. Addie added three more titles to the pile, because she liked to read to the babies. She'd read in the baby books, she'd bought early in her pregnancy, that it would encourage a love of words.

Finally, at the non-fiction shelves, she scanned. 'A Pictorial History of Tasmanian Bridges' caught her attention, and she added that as her single non-fiction choice, before returning to Jack. "Should I write the titles down?"

He smiled. "We've not actually had anyone borrow since the zombie situation arose. I think you'll be fine for now. Just remember to return them in a timely manner, I guess."

She stashed the pile of books into the baby bag and frowned as they spilled back out.

"Want to me carry that?"

Addie shook her head at Jack's query. There was no way she wanted him to know she was reading a steamy romance like Suzi Love's. She picked up one carrier and noted the baby lying safely within had dozed off again, then followed Jack out the door and to the car. Once the babies were settled, he returned to the door, engaged the locks, then joined her in the front seat.

CHAPTER 5

*J*ack yawned and stretched. He'd offered Addie access to his whole DVD library, and she'd tackled it with gusto. "I hadn't seen that movie," she offered, and he couldn't contain his smile.

In a lot of ways, anyone on the outside might think them a married couple. They sat on the lounge beside each other. They both held a baby who drowsed, the scent of baby powder winding around him.

"She's out for the count," he murmured, and rose smoothly, not wanting to jostle the child in his arms. "I'll go put her down—"

"Well, Fiona's out too. So, let's take both of them and get them settled. Then I think a last cup of tea before bed is in order."

They'd settled into a comfortable routine over the last four nights, as if they'd been doing it since Leanne and Fiona's birth.

Once the babies were settled, they moved into the kitchen. Addie set about filling the water jug with the filtered water they'd collected from the treatment plant, while he pulled the cups, tea bags and the bottled milk from the fridge.

"When do you expect the cattle to arrive?" Addie settled herself against the counter and watched him.

"The first two batches have already arrived. The family with the dairy cows has tracked down enough trucks to bring as many as they can. Another lot, who lived near them, are going to truck in beef cattle next week, at the same time. I've got the five guys we rounded up building the fences."

She bit her lip and screwed up her nose. "But they stink, don't they?"

He laughed. "I guess. But the supply of powdered milk is running low, so we have to do something. And the parks aren't exactly getting used, so it was the best option to fix all the issues there."

"I guess."

"You do realise, we have a small poultry farm on the northern end of the island which is why there's chicken meat and eggs, and the garden center in the middle of town is now being turned into a giant greenhouse for vegetables and there's a row of houses, going to be dozed to make garden beds. Soon, once we have everyone set up, we're going to be looking to allocate jobs. You'll be okay, though. With the babies and helping in the office—"

Addie squinted. "Well, I've got a brown thumb anyway, so I'm not much help."

He laughed. "They're also going to encourage people to grow veggies in their garden. I thought we might look at some basics? I mean, Fiona and Leanne will need to transition to solid food soon, won't they?"

"We've got a little while yet. The baby book I brought with me said not before four months and for many between six and nine months is normal."

He nodded. "Okay. But if we grow some ourselves... That has to be better, right?"

Her stare had him wondering if he'd overstepped the mark. The kettle whistled, and he thanked his lucky stars that she'd turned back. Not your kids, dickhead.

"What were you thinking? I mean, I don't know how long you want us here?"

On the tip of his tongue was the answer, "forever." He swallowed the words before they could slip out.

Jack accepted the tea she pressed into his hands and they both wandered out to the verandah that circled the house.

"Jack, I need to settle the kids. I know the other day you said to stay, but I can't just leech off you forever." He could see she'd thought long and hard about the words. He didn't have to like them, though.

"Give it time. When things settle down, we can talk about it, okay?" *That's right. Put it off for as long as possible. Get her used to being here and feeling at home.*

He shied away from the thought and slowly, bit-by-bit, the lights went out on the island as they had every night since the zombie situation had emerged.

"Why do you let the lights go out on the land," she asked.

"Saves electricity. We are still working on putting together enough batteries to create a backup for when the weather doesn't allow for harvesting."

"It must be hard, having the daily responsibility for the island. I couldn't do it."

He shifted uncomfortably. "I don't, really. I mean there are others..."

"Such as the MIA Mayor and his admin assistant?"

"Yeah, something like that." Now an additional concern bloomed. "But on that note, I haven't heard from either of them for several days." He wanted to kick himself for not twigging to that earlier. With the attack and loss of people, then trying to sort out the situation with the bridge, his concentration was split.

"What's worrying you, Jack?" She moved closer, so her shoulder brushed against his arm.

"The bridge. People's safety. Making sure we have enough resources to survive, you can take your pick."

"I'm sorry you have so many problems. I... We shouldn't be adding to them."

"You're not, Addie."

Silence stretched between them. She turned back to the view and drank quietly, as if giving him space to think.

This time when she turned back, she smiled. "I'm going to retire. Goodnight, Jack."

She left him there, but not before he realised, he'd rather her company. Except she needed her sleep, so once again he kept his mouth shut.

CHAPTER 6

*A*ddie typed the last item into her list then hit print, just as Jack stamped out into the large open space. "I've got the groups for the search set up and allocated the manpower as you requested. Thomas will be around later today, he sent a runner," she added before Jack could query how she knew, "and I've done up a set of instructions on how to alert us if they find the boat, the mayor and his assistant, Paula, are on."

Strain lines radiated from his mouth. She wished she could just smooth them away, but every fiber of her body warned that she might give in to the emotional tether between them.

"I've also hunted around and found the water bottles you told me about. They're filled and, in the kitchen, ready for the searchers."

"I... Thanks, Addie. You've done a wonderful job."

"Jack? Do you think they're still alive?"

He shrugged. "I don't know. It's been days. Normally, he can only take a day or two at most on the water. I mean, he has a cruiser, so it's all tricked out for longer trips. But he was supposed to come in..." He dragged his hand through his hair again. "I mean, he's unreliable, so I never know if he's going to turn up when he says he will."

"Okay, so what needs to be done in case, well, in case its worst case?" She felt awful, pushing, but if things had to be done, it was better to be prepared now, than having to rush around later.

"Someone needs to check on his dog."

"Dog? It's been how long?"

"It's a little thing—a chihuahua or something like that. Inside critter and no hair. He would have left food and water."

"Yes, fine, but what about toileting?"

His face blanked. "Oh. Shit."

"Exactly," she giggled and hoped it would lighten the surrounding tension.

"I need to go check on it. Maybe I should—"

"Bring it back here. Make sure you collect any bedding, food, leads and bowls. Oh, and toys."

"But Addie, there'll be no one—"

"I'll be here, along with Fiona and Leanne. When Thomas gets here, I'll let him in. Give him coffee or tea and a biscuit and he can wait in your office, or the library. Or even here."

Jack moved, heading back to his office, before emerging with his walkie talkie and keys. "I'll be back as soon as I can."

She nodded and turned back to the task she was attempting to complete, making her way through the lists of housing he'd dumped on her desk earlier in the day, and the number of bedrooms in houses, apartments, and units. She'd get this spreadsheet done as quickly as possible, then she'd find out how to get information on the families who were due to move and marry their needs to the properties available.

A little while later, a knock on the door echoed, and she rose, heading up the hall. When she noted a man in a police t-shirt, she carefully unlocked the door. "Thomas?"

"That's me." He held up an official-looking badge, and she squinted at it, then satisfied he was who he claimed to be, she moved out of the way allowing him to enter the building.

"Sorry, just being cautious. I'm Addie. Come on through."

He followed her down the hall and she settled him in a chair beside the babies. "Coffee or Tea?"

"Water would be great thanks."

She hurried over to the box of bottles and scooped one up, before handing it over.

"Yours?" He waved at the babies.

"My daughters, Fiona and Leanne." Something about the way he looked at them had her belly jittering.

"But not Jacks?" His gaze narrowed.

"No. My husband, Darcy died some months ago."

"I'm sorry for your loss," he muttered. But she wasn't sure he was. There was something off about the way he was watching her.

"Uh, thanks. Look, Jack said he'd be back soon. He's gone to get the mayor's dog."

Thomas nodded, and she turned her back, although completely aware that he was staring at her from the prickle on the nape of her neck.

"You're staying with Jack?"

He spoke again and Addie stilled, before swinging around. "Yes. He's kindly asked us to stay on."

If it was possible, Thomas' brows inched a little closer together. He opened his mouth, and she was worried what he'd ask this time when the sound of the door opening had her surging from her chair.

Jack came down the hall, a small dog under his arm and a large shopping bag full to the brim in his hand. "Oh good. Thomas, you've met Addie and the girls."

Thomas nodded.

The dog was handed to Addie while Jack disappeared into the kitchen with the bag.

"What are you...?"

"Mitzie doesn't look to have been let out. The house stinks and yes, there're presents all over the floor. She also had an empty water bowl."

"Mitzie?" Addie queried.

"The dog," Jack growled. "Looks like no one's been home." He laid down two bowls, one with meat and the other with water, and Mitzie wiggled in Addie's grasp. She leaned down and let the little dog go, after unhooking the lead attached to Mitzie's collar.

"So, I've got men here in the next hour. We need a plan." Thomas might be a man of few words, but those he had he used effectively, Addie thought snidely.

"Addie already has that planned. She's got water bottles for the searchers and a system of runners, for the land. On water, she's sending the boats out in teams." Jack's words of praise didn't go unnoticed by Thomas, whose mouth tightened. He might be a god on earth to look at, with his black hair and deep blue eyes, but he was also a dick, Addie thought.

"Yeah. A gem."

The dryness of Thomas' words must have impacted on Jack, because his brow now wrinkled too. "What does that mean?"

Thomas shrugged. "Nothing. Now let's see this plan."

Without a word, Addie handed over the sheaf of papers she'd prepared, along with the maps, with areas highlighted and the small team names she'd cobbled together with Jack's help. Then she turned back, sat down on her chair to gaze at the computer screen.

*J*ack didn't miss the way Thomas was acting around Addie. He'd talk to him as soon as they left the office, because he'd be damned if he'd allow her to be upset by his friend.

That there was enough of a reason to question what was happening, his heart whispered. Was there any way this could work...? She's got babies and is probably still grieving for her husband, urged his rational brain.

Once they settled in the police cruiser, Jack turned to Thomas. "What was that all about? With Addie?"

Thomas shrugged. "You're my friend. I hate to see you being taken advantage of by someone on the make."

"Advantage?" His mind nearly exploded at the ramifications of

Thomas' words. "First, Addie wanted to go to a hotel, but after the attack, I kept her at my place. She's got babies, and I want to make sure all three of them are safe. Second, the house is empty since Mum and Dad died. I'm racketing around in it, and there're only echoes and ghosts. And last, not that it's any of your business, but she's a hell of a cook and enjoys washing."

Thomas' brow quirked.

Jack's anger rose. "She's not taking advantage. That's what I want to do." As soon as the words flew from his mouth, he closed his eyes and groaned.

"Well. Fuck. I thought after Sarah, you'd never settle for a woman except—"

"I don't want to settle. Sarah was... She was not a mistake, exactly, but an experience. After she left, I thought I'd lost everything, but Addie? She wants nothing she doesn't earn, and she's not made any move on me. All she wants is for those babies to grow up safe."

"And you're hooked on them just as much as her." It wasn't a question.

"Yeah. Something like that."

"*Fuck.*"

Jack opened his eyes and looked to the growing mass of people waiting to hunt for the mayor at the old show grounds. "Yeah, that word is accurate, Tom. I'm fucked."

They climbed from the car and Thomas ran through the situation once everyone had gathered around and quieted.

"The mayor and his assistant Paula are missing. They've been gone several days, but most of you know how Lee is. He's difficult to track because he's notorious for not turning up. We think he took the boat, but the weather's been perfect. We need to check the beaches and check on the water. Jack has had lists and maps made up. You're to move in teams. No one is alone. We've got flare guns for each team, but only use them in the instance of a zombie attack."

People started to murmur, and Jack stepped up. "Yes, there was an attack on the hotel and yes, we lost people. We are fairly sure there is at least one on the island. It's why you don't leave your group.

Everyone here is armed. Use whatever force is necessary if they attack you. But try to stay within your zone. They do overlap so we don't miss any area. Boat teams, the same, but you've got multiple boats. If you find the boat or them, one boat comes ashore to make contact. The other stays where you found them."

Men and women nodded and agreed, and Jack was pleased that for all the mayor had been unpleasant, the people were still willing to search for him. Jack just hoped it was alive. If not... That didn't bear considering.

Water bottles, maps, flare guns and even sunscreen was handed out, and in an agreement, everyone would return to base at midday, unless he shot his gun into the air to get everyone back here as quickly as possible. He held the only red flare, so if shot, it would stand out.

They trailed away, and he settled on the bench of the picnic unit. Thomas settled opposite him.

"I'm sorry," Thomas muttered.

"You should be. She's not grasping or greedy. She's not looking for a free ride. Give her a chance."

Thomas nodded and Jack wondered why on earth his prickly friend had never found a woman, then snorted. Probably because he was so cynical. "What happened, Tom? Why did you change and start to see the worst in everyone?"

Thomas opened his mouth, then closed it again. Shook his head. "I just grew up," he finally answered.

They sat in silence until Thomas cleared his throat. "If he's dead, they need someone to lead them."

Jack smiled. "And you're just the man for the task."

Thomas' eyes almost popped out of his head. "Not me. You."

Surprise was a mild descriptor for the shock that threatened to overwhelm him. "Me? No way."

Thomas scoffed. "Right, says the man who had the search party called together. Who made the plans and gathered the supplies?"

"That was Addie," he explained.

"Under your direction?"

Jack shrugged.

"But really, someone will need to take charge. The Sarge can't and neither can I.

"We lost most of the possible leaders in the early days of the virus. They need someone to rely on. Someone capable of making decisions."

"There's others..." he was searching for the words when a white flare rose into the sky. "Shit!"

"It's coming from the water. Let's head down to the beach and see who and where."

Within moments they'd reached the sandy beach, and he dragged off his shoes and socks, searching the water. A small boat was zooming to shore, and he waited, hand cupping his brow.

Kelly, one of the fisherman's daughters, jumped from the still moving boat as it sidled to the shore. She waded out of the water, her long blonde hair dancing in the fine breeze. "We found the boat. They're... They must have been drinking, then fell overboard. The bodies... They were located floating near the boat. It's not good. Dave and Mick are going to bring them in. Leo is heading back to the mooring with the boat. The fish got to them. The bodies..." she shuddered, her gaze turning stormy. "There's the remains of a bottle of gin still on the table."

Jack stared at Kelly. He'd known her all his life, but right now, he could hate her. The information she carried was a weight on his chest. He didn't want the responsibility that Thomas had suggested should devolve to him.

"Thanks Kelly. Have your dad round up the stragglers. We'll head back to the meeting point, debrief the team."

Kelly nodded without looking at Thomas and retreated to the now idling boat.

"You're going to have to sort that out too," Jack told Thomas.

"It's already been done. Neither of us are interested in opening the old wounds."

Funny, Thomas had been quick to jump on Addie yet refused to accept a suggestion. If only Thomas could see both he and Kelly were hurting. He shrugged and followed Thomas back up to the show grounds.

*A*ddie yawned. The last two weeks had been busy. People had come and gone from the office, while Jack had fumed and fretted in alternate turns.

With the death of the mayor, it now fell to Jack to make the island community work. He was still searching for some way to demolish the bridge. The animals and new families arrived, and there'd been a major water drama when one of the pipes from the water plant had burst.

"Hey Addie, can you get Jack to check on the plans for the farm? The guy installing the shed and fencing isn't sure it would survive a cyclone, and are we still worrying about building codes? He needs to know by the end of today."

She scribbled the query down along with the name of the contact, before trying to marry the names to her list.

Since the information about the death of the mayor had spread, it seemed everyone needed a piece of Jack. Somehow it had been decided the best way to him was through her. In order to get a break long enough to even feed the babies, she'd taken to locking the door and hanging a meeting in progress sign on it. Not that is stopped them knocking until they realised no one was going to answer.

Meanwhile, Jack was at the police station, holed up with Thomas and the Sergeant.

Addie shuddered. After the encounter with Thomas, she'd be pretty much pleased never to have to meet with him again.

The rap on the door had her standing up and heading up the hall. "Back in the old days, I'd have been pleased if my pedometer captured all my steps," she muttered.

The woman standing there, in her mid-twenties with fine features, gray eyes and golden blonde hair was both tanned and tones. "Hi, you must be Addie. Jack sent this over for you and said to remind you to eat." She held out a paper bag, the aroma of fried fish ticking Addie's nose.

"Oh, wow. Thank you. Come in?"

The woman stared for a moment, then nodded. "I'd love to. I'm Kelly. Jack and I went to school together."

"Oh. Right."

Kelly wandered down the hall as if she'd been doing it all her life, then stopped, no doubt catching sight of the babies. "Oh my God... I heard you had twins. They're so pretty!" Today she'd dressed them in mint green romper suits with matching headbands. In the last week they'd somehow changed from newborn looking to rounded infants and were just beginning to try to push up off their belly with their arms.

"Would you like a drink?"

Kelly shook her head. "No thanks. I can't stay long. Dad and I brought in a catch this morning, and I asked Jack how many fish and he said check with you. Then he told me about the babies, and since I was cooking up anyway, I thought I'd bring it by straight away and meet you and them."

"Do you mind if I eat? They're nearly due for a feed and I don't get a chance to do much once they start."

Indeed, Jack had strong-armed Thomas to help him bring in an armchair so she could feed them both comfortably in the office space, and her nursing pillow lay ready along with fresh cloth nappies to catch any milky burps.

"Yes, eat."

Kelly got down on the floor and glanced back at Addie. "Do you mind if I pick them up?"

Addie shook her head. "No. Go for it."

She ate quickly while Kelly visited with Fiona, then Leanne. They rewarded the woman with gurgles and laughs. As soon as she finished, she asked Kelly if she'd watch them, headed for the bathroom then with her hands washed returned ready to feed them. Jack had returned with Thomas in tow, and Kelly had a distinct, 'get me out of here' look on her face.

"Thanks for the fish, Kelly, and for watching the twins. Maybe you'd like to stop by the house some day for a coffee? It would be nice to have friends, apart from Jack, here."

Kelly nodded and smiled and hurried for the door, while Addie trailed behind her. Once the woman had left the building, Addie locked the door again.

Before Jack could retreat into his office with Thomas, she called his name. "I've got a bucket load of messages and people need answers. Some are urgent."

His face clouded. "Okay. I need to do this first with Thomas, then I'll get to them. You're going to...?" He indicated to the babies, and she knew what he was asking.

"Yes."

"Okay. Sign on the door?"

Addie nodded, and Jack retreated into his office, shutting the door.

CHAPTER 7

Jack fumed. He had better things to do than sit here, shooting the breeze with groups of people, but he also understood the people needed stability. Since Lee's death, there was a marked increase in concerns from those remaining on the island.

There'd been several families who were agitating about leaving. He couldn't and wouldn't stop them, though he did have concerns about their safety.

"Jack, Nina, and Sam plan to leave in the morning. But it's dangerous out there." Carl whined.

"It is dangerous everywhere. But if they wish to leave, they can. Even more importantly, I need them to know that if they want to return, they can. But we need to discuss the families that are going to relocate to the houses on the north side of the island."

Carl frowned. "So, the safety of Nina, Sam and the three kids is lower on the priority list?"

"That's not what I said, Carl. You know I'd prefer they stay. They're your family, but even so, this is still a democratic country."

Carl stood up. "And who voted you in charge?" he snarled.

It took every ounce of restraint to control the urge to yell at the older man before him. "No one. But no one else wanted the job, Carl. Unless you want to stand?"

The man faltered, his face falling. "No."

"Right. So, if you can't talk them into staying, how do you think I will?" He sighed. "To be honest, things aren't even safe here. We haven't found the missing zombie and there's been two near misses, Carl. I need to move people as soon as possible so we can ensure their safety. To do that, I need your assistance."

"I haven't had a chance to look at the requests yet," Carl answered with a sulky tone, head dropping down.

"Carl, you've had the information for nearly a week." But it was useless to push. There had to be another way. "What about if I bring Addie out here? She can meet the families herself, get the details and make the allocations then?"

"I can do it. I will do it. When I'm ready," the old man groused.

"I can only give you until Saturday. If you haven't got the information to me, I'm going to have to go over your head and direct to the families. I don't want to step on your toes, but you've stepped up as the organizer for this zone. People are relying on you." He tried to keep the words calm but firm, knowing how ornery the man could be.

Carl's face turned red, then white. "You just want to get rid of me, like you did with Lee. I know what this is all about—"

Jack's mind went blank for a moment. *'You just want to get rid of me, like you did with Lee.'* Did Carl really think he'd been behind Lee and Paula's untimely death? Obviously so, if the ranting of the old man was anything to go by.

"I had nothing to do with their deaths, Carl. I can tell you that I was nowhere near when they died. I did raise concerns several days after their disappearance."

"And I heard the maps you handed out meant they were found quickly. Isn't that interesting?" the man sneered.

"I'm not going to argue with you. I will tell you, on the good book as my mother would say, that I had nothing to do with it. If you have so much dissatisfaction with my actions and leadership, you can choose to step down. It's your choice, Carl. You can be part of the problem, or you can be part of the solution."

That stopped Carl short. His mouth opened like a floundering fish, then he closed it again.

"Carl?"

"You're a fucking dangerous fool. I won't be part of this. Find someone else to fill the roll and be your fucking lackey!" He threw the folder at Jack, who watched the man and felt only pity. He'd once been a banker and investor, important and respected in the region. When the businesses didn't perform, he took them over, hired people to make them work, and his wealth had grown. Now, he eked out his existence, in a world where money didn't talk, making him just like everyone else.

Jack wondered if that was the root cause of his bitter, caustic nature. But then again, maybe it wasn't. Maybe he was truly just an asshole at heart.

What did concern Jack, though, was how many others thought he'd orchestrated Lee's death? He'd enough connections to ensure the story stuck like mud.

A woman in her early thirties, he guessed, came running over, waving her hand. "Mr. Fredericks? Mr. Fredericks! Wait!" She hurried, the squeak of her sensible shoes on the linoleum floor a strange juxtaposition to the sharp tension on her face.

He stilled, wondering what new disaster was about to befall them all. It felt like, since he'd taken over, things were failing, falling apart and generally disorganised.

"Yes?"

"I'm Ellie Weintraub, and my family has asked several times about the relocation. Carl only said it was being held up and his hands tied. We aren't the only ones. We want to move and soon, but you won't make the allocations. Why is that?"

Her fingers were curled around the original flyers he'd printed up after Lee had finally agreed to his plans to streamline the residential situation. Now it was his turn to stare, open-mouthed. "I... That's not quite right. Carl has had the paperwork concerning how to allocate the apartments for a week. I was here trying to get the information out of him."

She blinked. The frustration making way for understanding. "Really? Stupid fool of a man. My uncle never used the brains God gave him." There was a bite in her tone.

"Your uncle?"

"Unfortunately, so. Not that he recognizes our side of the family. We could inherit the crown jewels and we'd still be dirt beneath his feet," she muttered. "Mum reckoned Carl had a sense of entitlement that spanned three cricket grounds end-to-end!"

Jack sputtered at her dry description of the man. "Right. So, he's stepped down from the regional organizer post. Would you be interested in the role?"

She squinted. "Why?"

"I need someone who can think clearly, speak their mind and advocate for the people from here. You strike me as someone who could probably fill that bill."

"Maybe. I'd need to talk with my brother, sister and kids," she hedged, "but I am interested."

"Would that pose a problem, following on from Carl?" He waited.

She shook her head. "Not really. Most people from around here know the story. Carl was demanding access to his inheritance and grandfather sat him on his arse. Told him he wouldn't get anything if he kept pushing. Carl didn't listen and grandfather wrote him out of the will. Told him he'd have to work for his future, since my dad was already working the farm." Ellie shrugged. "Dad gave up school at seventeen, because grandfather had a heart attack. Carl could have done the same, but he didn't like the hours, the dirty hands and clothes. He was difficult, according to dad, his entire life. He's annoyed a lot of people over a whole range of things in the last fifty years. Crowed over their defeats and missteps and always found a way to make it work for him. Not many will regret that he stood aside."

Jack nodded. "And his daughters, Ellie and Sam?"

"Oh, they'd had enough of him ruling their life. That's why

they're planning to leave, not that I guess that's the story he spun you, right?"

"No. He said it was to do with Lee's death."

Now she snickered. "That's bloody rich! He and Lee were like peas in a pod. They'd known each other for a long time, and both traded off the 'old family' title, not to mention the financial rewards Carl helped him amass. Your family has been here how long?"

He did some quick arithmetic in his head. "Uh, nearly twenty-two years."

"There you go. Still a newcomer to the island by Carl's standards."

"Something like that. But if your family agrees, you'll take the role?"

She nodded slowly. "Yeah. I will. I'm trusted and I want better for our area."

Carl had left the walkie talkie behind, so Jack grabbed it, thrust it into her hand. Then fished around in the box Carl had left in the old building for the folder holding the sheaf of paper detailing accommodation and details of each independent unit. "Get hold of people. See if you can fill this out by Saturday. If you can't, I'll bring Addie over. We can set up appointments. After we get that sorted, she wants to sort out the schools. Get the kids back to their education as quickly as possible."

Ellie nodded. "Okay. I can do that."

⁂

*J*ack was due home any moment, and Addie fretted. What to cook for dinner? She needed vegetables and, on looking in the cupboards for tinned options, found it a little spare. Tonight, she'd hoped to make a nice mild chili and to set up a slow cooker dahl with naan bread. She'd found the freeze-dried yoghurt starter at what had once been the health food shop and snapped it up along with the sourdough starter.

But the cupboards were growing increasingly bare, and shopping with the twins was a trial.

The sound of a car, the closing of the gate, had her blood thrumming in a way she now associated with Jack.

Yet, much as she might be drawn to him, he clearly didn't feel the same to her. In fact, it almost felt like he was treating her like a sister or friend.

Entering the friend-zone meant absolutely no chance of a relationship. She sighed and shoved those thoughts aside.

When he entered, she smiled her welcome. "I'm so pleased your home. I need to pop out, grab some supplies before the stores shut up." She snatched the keys from his hand. "The twins should sleep for a while; the washing is dry and folded and I dropped your things on the bed. When I get home, I'll start dinner." Addie had no intentions of giving him time to remonstrate and hurried out the door.

She opened the gates with the device he kept in the car, turned the ignition and reversed out of the driveway. Thankfully, there was little to no traffic on the island, and it occurred to her, at some point, they'd likely run out of petrol.

"I'll have to raise that with him," she muttered and drove quickly to the area where the markets would be found.

With the door locked, she hurried for the shop and let herself in. "Hi! I've just come for some supplies."

"Welcome to the market," said the girl on the counter wearing the name Sarah. She waved as Addie scooped up a basket and headed up the aisle. Tinned beans, potatoes, tomatoes and peas went into the basket along with lentils. Some flour and yeast came next, and she was reaching for the milk powder when she heard a sound that chilled her core.

The low moaning dirge of the undead.

"Oh, my god!" The girl on the desk screamed and Addie was frozen still. Unable to move or even make her mind think.

"No!" the girl screamed again, and the sound of a crash echoed in her brain.

Another moan joined the first. Her mind whirred. More than one and they were locked in a shop. She bit her lip and looked up, noting the mirror on the wall. *Three! Three zombies.*

"Sarah, run!" Addie bellowed. The front door was obstructed by the big shuffler, but the back door might be an option. "Come on!" Unaware that the basket remained slung over her arm, she made her legs move. Pumped them and headed to the back. Large shelves stacked here and there, with a few boxes stacked on each one.

Sarah shuffled beside her, babbling uselessly. "Where do we go? They're going to get us!"

The door wasn't easy to see. "How do we get out of here?" She demanded.

"The door doesn't work. We don't have the keys. It doesn't unlock!"

Addie tried to come up with a workable plan, aware the shufflers were heading in their direction. "The shelves. Do they move?" They scurried out of sight behind the first set.

"No."

"Fuck." They were trapped. The only way out was to go... She looked up. There were exposed rafters, and they appeared to be heavy metal. "Up."

It wasn't a great option, but as far as she knew, shufflers didn't think and couldn't climb. She shoved the girl at the shelves. "Start climbing," she ordered and hurried to a spot beside her.

"But..."

"Climb Sarah or we're dead." She dropped the basket and started clambering, glad she wore shorts even if the wood edges of the raw shelves scraped her skin, heart thrumming wildly.

Fear urged her to move as fast as possible and they reached the top shelf. "Into the rafters, Sarah."

The girl stared. "I'm... I'm scared of heights!" She squeaked.

Heart in her throat as the zombies were now headed in their direction, she grabbed onto Sarah and shook her. "More scared of heights or zombies?"

The girl, white faced, nodded, tears streaming. "You're... You're right."

Sarah was shorter than Addie, so she boosted her. Hands were now reaching for her, and she reached out. "Pull me up, Sarah."

The girl grunted, and with a jump, Addie's hand closed around the rafter.

It groaned, which terrified Addie. What if it gave? They'd die and her twins would grow up without her. They'd be orphans. Jack would look after them, she was pretty sure, given how much he was involved now in their day-to-day care, but without their mother... The one person who could tell them about their father... Unfair, her heart screamed. But life sucked in their current reality. There was a chance of survival, her brain reminded her. She just had to hang on.

"I'm... They're going to get us," moaned Sarah.

Addie felt another moment of panic and beat it back. "Not if we keep still. But we need help. We need to get someone's attention."

"How," whined Sarah piteously.

"We scream. We scream really loud and hope someone hears us."

CHAPTER 8

Jack answered the imperious peal from his walkie talkie. "Thomas?"

"Where are you?" There was a thick tension in his voice and Jack's guts twisted.

"At home. With the twins."

"Where's Addie?"

"She went down to the market to get supplies. Why? What's going on?"

Thomas swore. "Shit! Because there're zombies in the market. We can hear someone screaming, but getting in... It's difficult."

"Thomas..." He didn't know what to say. Addie had become his mainstay. The rock. He came home to her every night, enjoyed her wit and company. They'd even gone fishing on Saturday, perched on the old jetty while the twins slumbered in the pram he'd found for her use.

His mouth felt thick, and words blocked up in his throat along with his heart. His guts freezing with terror.

"We're going in, but Jack, we don't know their situation. We only know there's more than one. Cornering them... It's dangerous."

Heat stung his eyes. He knew what Thomas was saying. If she'd been bitten, she would likely become one of them. The shuffling undead. The reality he could lose the woman who'd banished his loneliness, lancing through him like a knife.

He wanted to be there, but the babies... He couldn't leave them. He couldn't take them into the situation either. "I... Fiona and Leanne."

"Stay with them. If we get her out, if she's alive, we'll bring her home. Unless—"

"She's bitten." He finished the sentence.

"Yeah. Then we can't risk it."

He slumped to the ground, holding onto the walkie talkie after Thomas signed off. He could see the babies sleeping in the cot, and for the first time since the death of his parents, he prayed.

He prayed for Addie's survival, for his soul and the strength to face forever alone with only Addie's babies to walk beside him.

They slept on, unaware of the pain and terror that gnawed at his brain and heart.

Silent tears dripped down his face, but he was too chilled to notice them as he huddled waiting for news.

It felt like an eternity before he heard the squelch of the radio. "Jack?"

"Ye..." He cleared his throat. "Yeah?"

"She's okay. Scared and shaky, but okay. She got the girl from the shop up into the rafters. That's who we heard screaming."

The sluggish flow of his blood hastened. "She's okay?"

"Yeah. We got the zombies, but there were three, Jack. Where there's that many, there's usually more. We need that bridge dealt with before they work out how to get through the gates."

Jack scrubbed his eyes, swiping away the evidence of his tears. "Yeah. I just... I can't find anything that will give me the information on how to create an explosive."

"We won't survive if they attack in numbers," Thomas warned and once again, Jack felt the weight of responsibility.

"I know."

Thomas sighed, and the echo came through the air like a squelch. Loud. Fiona stirred. "We'll be there soon."

Jack shoved himself off the floor. She'd be wanting to see the babies. Probably cold. He'd make her a tea... He shook his head. She'd probably want something stronger. His dad's drink cabinet hadn't been opened since his death. Tonight, he wanted something stiff and strong, and maybe so would Addie.

He heard the car. Saw it drive in, followed by another vehicle. Thomas stepped out of Addie's car, and she followed, hugging a bloody basket in her arms, hunched in on herself.

She moved slowly, faltering on the steps, and Thomas' arm slipped around her.

At the top of the steps, she stilled. Looked up. Their gazes meshed.

"Addie," he whispered, and she moved, dropping the basket with a thud and diving into his waiting arms.

Thomas caught his attention. "I'll need to talk to her tomorrow. Tonight, look after her. It was her thinking that saved them both." Thomas shook his head. "How they fucking survived," he mumbled and hurried down the steps.

"Thomas?" His friend stopped at the bottom of the stairs, turned with a question in his eyes. "Thanks. For everything." It wasn't nearly enough, but for now, it would do.

Addie shook in his embrace and Jack closed his eyes, thanking God, the universe and every possible deity that she'd survived.

He inhaled her scent, and his world once more began to rotate on its axis.

*A*ddie couldn't get a grip on her emotions. While they'd hung there, she'd focused on attracting help, keeping Sarah from giving up. Staying beyond the questing hands of the zombies.

Now it was over, she felt like she was falling apart. Jack held her tight, whispering words she couldn't understand over the crying jag, but whatever he said, the words didn't matter because he held her close. For now, she'd be thankful.

How long they stood there, she had no idea but the wail of first one, then a second angry baby cry split the air.

"Fiona. Leanne." She tugged away and Jack let her go, but it felt like he'd hung on a moment longer than necessary.

"They slept. Now go to them, they need you."

She turned toward them, stilled, then turned. *I nearly died, and I'll always regret this if I don't take the chance.* Shifting onto tiptoes, she kissed him. On the mouth.

Addie felt his shock, the way his body stilled, muscles locking. She backed away, but he reached out, caught her shoulders with tight fingers that dug deep and hauled her back.

The kiss wasn't safe or chaste. It was wild and hot, with his mouth opening over hers.

Shock coursed. He... He wanted her?

His body was hot, burning her, urging her to deepen the connection.

Addie skipped away, the wails of the babies demanding her presence couldn't be denied.

J ack waited in the kitchen, having retrieved the basket Addie had brought home. He lined the tins up in the cupboard and hunted through the freezer. A bag of frozen chips had languished forgotten by his mother.

The memory of her complaints of unhealthy food had him choking down a sob.

His emotions felt fragile, and he couldn't even begin to understand how she felt. He'd forced the second kiss, the first whetting his appetite for more.

The one thing it did clarify was she wanted him too.

The skin of his face burned, while he grabbed out the air fryer he'd bought his mother last Christmas. She'd stashed it at the back, stating that fried foods were unhealthy. He'd laughed it off at the time, determined he'd change her mind.

He dumped two good handfuls into the tray before turning to the fish they'd caught together. In a drawer Jack found tinfoil and garnished the fish, topping it with herbs and dotted butter before sliding it into the oven.

By the time she emerged, the babies bouncing happily, the meal was almost ready to serve.

"You cooked?" She smiled shyly.

"My repertoire isn't extensive, but I thought you'd appreciate the break." He slid the food onto plates and carried it out.

By unspoken agreement, neither discussed what happened at the market. That he left for later, when they could sit, and he could hold her. After the babies were settled in their cot.

He'd poured a glass of white wine. Stocks were getting low on the island, but he considered tonight it was more akin to a health tonic than an indulgence.

Once the meal was finished, she helped carry the plates to the kitchen and wash up.

He changed the babies while she fed them. There was a sense of expectation in the air, as if something momentous was gathering just beyond sight.

With the babies settled and asleep, he dragged her close. "I couldn't believe it when Thomas called and told me what happened at the market. I felt like something inside me was going to die. But I have to tell you, I want to know. I need you to tell me."

"It was awful, Jack. I'd stocked up on the vegetables and was about to finish up when I heard them. Looking up, I saw them in the mirror. Sarah must have been terrified, and I know I was. It's funny, you think you'll know how to react, but in that instant, it's not just fight and flight. There's a third word—freeze. I heard her scream, and that made me move. We got into the storeroom, but the door is stuck, and the keys missing. There wasn't anywhere else to go but up, so we did. Then we made as much noise as possible to get attention."

He knew she left out the terror, he'd seen it on her face

after the fact. Felt the way she trembled in his arms. "I'm so sorry, sweetheart. I'd rather you never had to experience the fright."

"Me too. But I have to tell you, Jack. If it wasn't for that, I'm not sure I'd have kissed you. In my mind, I was sure a mother with kids wasn't what you wanted."

"But you still kissed me," he pointed out, feeling his chest puff out with satisfaction.

"I'd nearly died. It was one thing I'd have regretted, and I have to tell you, I wasn't disappointed."

He laughed and felt the rumble of her laughter as she snuggled into his embrace.

"Come outside with me. We'll have a drink; I'll pop on some music, and I want to dance with you."

"Like this?" She indicated to the shorts and t-shirt she wore.

"Especially like that," he answered. "Grab the wine and pour, while I find some music."

His parents had been dancers, attending the regular old-time nights at the local hall, and while he hadn't been in their league, he still wasn't a slouch.

She hurried inside and he dug out an old album, placed it on the turntable while the strains of a waltz crackled and popped. Music of his childhood, he thought with fondness.

When she returned, Addie popped the glasses on the outdoor table and moved into his embrace. Their bodies moving and swaying with synchronicity.

"Addie?" he murmured in her ear.

"What?" Her voice was breathless.

"I want to kiss you."

She turned her face, eyes shining and with care, he lifted both hands, so he could frame her face. Their lips touched. Last time the caress had been wild, but this was different. Soft and sweet but aching with promise.

She sighed and softened in his arms as he allowed her to still, to move closer, molding her body against his.

His body ached with lust and something more. Not yet, he warned his mind and body. Tonight, wasn't for taking.

Their tongues tangled, and he tasted the sweetness of her essence. Felt the way her breasts mashed to his chest, the long line of her legs as she stretched up. Her arms wound around his midsection, holding him as close as possible with clothing separating their skin.

Jack pulled back, gazed into her eyes. "Addie, I want you." He needed to give her time to understand, he wasn't asking for simple sex. Hell yes, he wanted that too, but at the middle of it all, he wanted her heart too.

"Jack, I'm yours," she whispered.

"I want more than tonight, Addie. I want us to take this slow. To be committed to growing a relationship. I know you've got Fiona and Leanne and I promise I won't do anything to hurt them, but I want to explore this thing between us. I want to be sure when we explore the physical, that you're sure."

The words weren't right. They didn't quite convey what he wanted them to, but it was all he had.

She cupped his cheek. "I know. But today...? That could happen anytime, and it's one of the things we both fear. I want to know Leanne and Fiona are cared for."

He opened his mouth to settle her fears, but the soft pads of her fingers slid over his lips.

"Shh. I know, you'll care for them like your own. I've seen how you love them already. I have no fears on that count. But Jack, they're babies and a huge responsibility. Most men would run away at this point, screaming."

His chest puffed out. "I'm not most men, Addie."

"No. You're Jack. The man I will take to lover one day soon. The man who I want to be the father to my girls and what I'm saying really badly is, I want a relationship. I want love and to live beside you. Your equal. Your lover. I know what you're saying. I agree, we need time to get to know one another, but time is fleeting, too. I don't want to regret never having loved you."

They kissed again and the bubble of warmth in his chest grew.

Time passed, and they swayed together now. And when the album ended, she crooked her finger. "Come stay with me tonight. Hold me."

Her voice was the call of a Siren. He couldn't deny her request. He followed her to the bedroom, watched as she settled in the bed, and he climbed in beside her. She scooted closer and rest her head on his shoulder, and soon enough they both fell asleep.

CHAPTER 9

*J*ack insisted Addie remain home the next day. He was needed in the office; but she was to rest.

The babies at almost three months now had a clear routine, so she prepared the food she'd planned for the night, a tasty dahl which she placed into the slow cooker. The naan bread she'd make tonight.

With the washing up-to-date and the house sparkling, Addie settled with the books she'd borrowed from the library two weeks previously. The Suzi Love looked enticing but given the fact she wasn't 'sleeping' with Jack yet and the raunchy cover of the book, Addie popped that one aside. "Later on. When we're into the sexy," she promised herself.

The next, the latest Keri Arthur would require her to commit to reading it in chunks and her mind couldn't settle to something like that, so instead she settled for the history book.

Leafing through it, Addie marveled at the beauty of the island state. She'd seen documentaries, but the vibrant colors still startled. By the time she reached the Derwent River, she had no idea of the shock that waited.

The river was wide and connected the two sections of Hobart, with some thirty percent unable to access the greater Hobart area after the ship, Illawarra, collided with several pylons, destroying the Tasman Bridge.

Now Addie stood and hurried to the verandah. In the distance, she could see the span of the bridge linking Hopeworth Island to the mainland. "I wonder..." she murmured.

Glancing to the clock, she noted it was nearly lunch. "He'll be home soon." She scurried to the kitchen and made a quick soda bread loaf. With a lentil soup, it would be filling and healthy.

She heard the car as her blood pounded through her veins, waiting with anticipation.

Reaching to top of the stairs, she met him with a kiss. "Hey you."

"Hey back, gorgeous. How are my favourite babies," he whispered against her mouth?

"Sleeping, right now. But I have something I want to show you." Addie grabbed his hand and towed him to the lounge. She scooped up the book and shoved it into his hands.

"I like books, but still," he laughed.

"No. Read it."

He frowned but followed her instruction. Then his gaze lifted to hers. "You're amazing."

"Will it work?"

Jack inhaled, "I don't know. But I think this is a plan we can consider. If we can find the right kind of vessel..." He shook his head. "And all this time, what we were looking for was in the library."

Addie grinned. "Never know when you're going to find some nugget in a book."

He tugged her tight. "Damn straight. But let's get some lunch and—"

"Already done. I've got a lentil soup and soda bread in the oven. Come on into the kitchen while I serve it up."

*J*ack couldn't conceive that something so simple might just be the answer they'd missed. A barge and/or large ship. Drive it into the pylons with enough force. The question was how much speed was necessary to exert the required amount of duress on the concrete.

He ate lunch slowly. Lentil soup wouldn't have been something he'd have even considered before the virus, but Addie made it tasty. "This is great, sweetheart. You're a damn good cook."

"I wanted to attend culinary school but couldn't afford it. I was working as a barista when I met Darcy. Saving up for college, then I got pregnant."

"Do you regret...?" It was hard to push the words out, because he knew she loved those babies, as did he.

"No. I mean, I love them and don't regret them at all. Just, in a perfect world, I'd have waited until I was older. Settled and established. Darcy was... He was like lightning. Hot and wild. I let myself be dragged along, but I honestly can't see that what we had was the kind of relationship that would make it to the 'death do we part' kind. We didn't marry in a church, and I'm kind of glad about that. It would have been, I don't know, not a lie, but—"

"Something you might have regretted later on?"

Addie swirled her spoon in the soup before looking up. "You understand?"

He nodded. "Olivia, the girl I was seeing, she would have been the same. I was trying to stash money, so I could buy the right kind of house in the right location. She wanted a man who could give her lifestyle. The kind with a capital 'L'." Now he grimaced. "I'd bought the ring. A big flashy diamond and planned to give it to her that weekend when I found out she was cheating on me. I never found out who with. By then, it didn't matter." He shrugged, but when she reached her hand across the table, he took it, rubbed his thumb over the knuckles of her fingers. "I gave up the unit where I was renting and moved home. To lick my wounds, I guess, initially. Besides, my parents needed me. Thomas had returned home too, and he was the one who told me about Olivia. He had photos of her and the other man. He never showed me the face, and I never asked."

"She was stupid and vacuous. No real woman would give up someone like you. A caring man who would do anything for the woman he loves. Her loss is my gain."

He laughed at the ferocity in her words and the scowl on her face. "I don't regret it, Addie. It brought me you and the babies." He meant every word. If he'd had to do it again, he would.

Her eyes shone with emotion. "We should finish our lunch," Addie admonished, but he could tell she was pleased with his words.

*A*ddie brushed her hair, then stopped. Scanned the woman she saw in the mirror. Her breasts were larger, her body rounded unlike before the twins. Her hair shone and her skin was sun kissed. Tugging on the silk robe she'd found in the cupboard; she loved the feel of it sliding over her skin. She touched the lapel and smiled, because she had plans for tonight.

The glint of gold on her finger melted her smile. Darcy. She'd been in love with love when they'd married, but it hadn't been that emotion that couldn't be ignored. The need to be right for the other person.

She'd been so happy that day, but now she knew a lot of that was because of the babies.

"What I feel now is different." It wasn't wrong to acknowledge that. Wearing Darcy's ring while with Jack was wrong, though. An indelible truth she couldn't ignore. Making the decision, Addie reached for her finger and removed the band. It was the right decision to slip it off. This was her girls' legacy, she guessed. A ring seemed a paltry thing. A tiny reminder of a life lived, but their existence wasn't easy or straightforward since the virus. She slid the piece onto the small jewellery plate of the dressing table.

"Darcy, you will always be a part of me. A part of our girls, but it's time to let you go. To move on." A small breeze eddied through the room and slid across her cheek like the caress of a hand. Whimsically she wondered if it was his final goodbye, then laughed at the ridiculous notion.

Lightness filled her and with a nod to herself in the mirror, Addie turned, headed for the man waiting down the hall. The one she had every intention of being with for the rest of her life.

CHAPTER 10

*J*ack watched as Addie entered the room. There was something different about her. As if she'd gained a confidence she hadn't carried about her, beforehand.

Reaching for him, she smiled, and the look in her eyes melted his guts. "Addie?"

"Tonight, Jack. I know we need time to get to know each other better, but tonight I want you. All of you. I want you to love me." She reached out, cupped his face, as if searching for a hint of his emotions. "I removed my wedding ring, Jack."

The words were a Siren's call. His knees shook, and he tugged her close. His body hot and hard with the utterance of those simple words.

The kiss was incendiary. Scorching, branding and far more hauntingly perfect than anything that came before. His hands slid down her body, cupping her sweetly rounded backside and anchoring them both.

"Jack," she whispered, her hands finding the first button of his shirt and releasing it. Then the next. The sounds of pops loud in his ears.

"Slow down, gorgeous. We have all night."

"I don't want to, Jack. I'm burning for you. Feel," she offered and slid the silky fabric of her wrap from one shoulder.

He scrabbled hard. Tonight, had to be perfect, because as far as he was concerned, this was the last first time. For both of them.

Tugging the shoulder back up, he levered away, just enough to catch sight of the confusion and embarrassment that flashed over her features. "Oh..." Addie's hands released him, flew to her burning cheeks. "I'm..." she gulped. "I'm sorry. I've pushed too hard and fast." Now her words turned into babble.

He covered her hands with his, "No. You're not rushing me too fast. I just want tonight to be perfect for you. I want this to be something you remember forever, Addie, and in the years to come, I want you to burn at the memory of the two of us together."

Her eyes sheened. "I'm not too forward?" Her voice took on a lost whisper and while the understanding he'd handled it poorly twisted in his belly, he shook his head.

"No. But I wanted moonlight and music. Wine. Soft touches and whispered words for you. You deserve nothing but the best, my Addie. Did I read it wrong?"

She trembled. "No, but... I want you tonight."

"And so, I shall be yours. But let's take our time. Build the feeling. Come on, let's go outside and enjoy the moonlight." He took her hand and towed her out, settled her on a chair, then moved inside to grab two glasses and the bottle of champagne his parents had bought on his birth. The one they'd always teased was kept for his never-going-to-happen wedding.

He stashed the bottle in the freezer, then hunted in the cupboard. At the very back was a box of after-dinner mints, left over from last Easter. His mother strictly rationed all such treats, and he smiled. Wondering if somehow, she knew one day, he'd be looking for them. He laughed at the whimsical notion.

He returned outside, after making a side trip to the record player, and found a soulful sax album, and slid a copy of lounge music beside it, ready if he needed to drag out the night a little more.

Addie was standing at the railing, looking off into the night. "It's beautiful here. I can see what it must have been like before all the houses were built."

Not that the house was by any means built out. Most of the older properties had been sold in the past year. His parents had been fending off developers wanting to get their hands on the prime waterfront property, the blocks next door now vacant—the houses dozed in readiness. "They planned to build apartments."

"Such a shame. Houses like this, they're full of history. Love. The stories and ghosts of those who came before."

"The house is over a hundred years old. Built by a sea captain for his wife and family. Mum and Dad bought it from the granddaughter who'd had terminal cancer. She'd given strict instructions that anyone wanting to buy it had to pass her scrutiny. I don't remember, but mum and dad said they took me with them to meet her. She'd apparently been taken by a family wanting it. Back then, Mum and Dad were still trying for a sibling, but it never took again. It was the three of us and this beautiful house."

"I can feel the love in it." She rubbed a hand over the railing, "though I think it needs oiling, the exposed wood."

"I had oil in the garage and planned to do it the week that everything changed." He settled his hands on her shoulders. Felt the suppleness of her muscles and rubbed. Kneaded while she continued to face away. "Tell me about growing up."

"My parents were hippies. Not the closet, pretend I'm mainstream kind, but the all-in variety. They wore hemp clothing, made their own sandals, and professed modern medicine was little more than a government conspiracy." She laughed; the sound tiny. "I guess they were a kind of right. Anyway, they moved to a commune when I was seventeen and able to get a job. I was a little different. I wanted a home, family and a dog."

"Two point three kids and a mortgage," he murmured the statistics.

"Something like that." She covered one of his hands with her own. "I told them about Darcy and the babies. They were planning to come up and visit, but Mum... She went gathering one day, came back and she'd been bitten. She turned and got Dad. He rang me before he... passed. Told me he loved me. I don't know what happened to my sister Celeste. She took off when I was nine."

"She was older?"

"Hmm," her head slid back against his shoulder, and he noted her eyes had closed. "Twelve years older and hated the 'nuts and berries lifestyle' as she called it. We lost touch a long time ago."

He kissed the top of her head, and Addie sighed. The sound full of longing. His body ached for her, but he refused to rush her tonight. He started the slow massage of her shoulders again, aware that she swayed slightly to the music, every move a caress to his body.

"You're beautiful, Adrienne. The moonlight shines on your hair, making it glow and kisses your skin."

She moved, slowly turning in his embrace, her eyes shining. "You have a magic way of speaking, Jack. The words fill me up and make me happy, your touch is the sweetest torture and all I want to do is love you."

A lump of emotion obstructed his breath, and he carefully placed his hand in her hair and pulled her close, so their lips touched. They were soft pillows he wanted to sink into, and when they opened, his eyes closed, his mind overloading with sensations. The scent and taste of the woman in his arms, the sweetest ambrosia.

Her hands rose, circled his neck, fingers tangled in his hair as she urged him to deepen the kiss.

He nibbled at her lips before settling to explore, finding her jawline and dotting it with kisses that had her stretching, wordlessly asking for more.

"God, Addie, I'm on fire for you. I want to last, but I might explode."

She laughed a little, the husky sound sending tremors through his body. Her hand settled on his chest, sliding down slowly like the sweetest torture before resting on the bulge at his groin.

"You'll last, Jack," she breathed as he found the length of her neck, his tongue finding supple flesh to worship.

Now she bedeviled him. Her fingers finding his belt and he felt it release. His hand dropped, covered hers. Jack opened his eyes, "Wait."

He stepped back, and she mewled. He reached for the single piece of fabric that, he guessed, held her gown together. With a tug, it came free, and the gown opened to reveal her nakedness. Heavy breasts, full of milk and deep rosy nipples, pouting her arousal.

She moved, but once again he stopped her. "Tonight, this is my pleasure," he whispered, and traced the blue veins radiating to the areola. "Amazing. The first time I saw you, you fed the babies from your body. The sight was natural, and I was drawn to you. The Madonna and her children."

With a gentle, soft move, he cupped a breast, amazed at the perfection of her body. He brushed a thumb over the pink tip, and she gasped, body locking and eyes closing. Her mouth formed a perfect 'O.'

Fingers trailed to the valley between the peaks and shadows played over her belly, still rounded from her pregnancy and he dropped to his knees before the exquisite sight. With his tongue, he found the depression of her navel and flicked in. She groaned and arched, hands gripping the rails, knuckles white while her legs shook.

Standing, he took her hand and pulled her inside, leaving the doors open, a tangy breeze sliding over them.

In the middle of the lounge, he stopped. "Stay here," he ordered and tugged the many pillows from the chairs, making a soft divan-like bed, then drew her down. Now his hands shook as he pulled his shirt free, uncaring that buttons popped.

Addie watched, one knee bent, the soft robe gaping and totally unconcerned about her near nudity as her gaze devoured him.

When she returned to his embrace, skin sliding against skin, he could almost swear he heard angels singing, those hot nubs grazing his now sensitive flesh.

"Jeez Addie." He captured her mouth again, tugging at the lower lip, while sliding his hands to juncture of her thighs. The rasp of hair a counterpoint to the hot, wet sex it hid.

He played his fingers over her dewy flesh, slid within, and she arched off the floor. "Jack," she panted. "I want you."

He smiled to see the blind way she groped for him. "Soon. Let me learn what pleases you first."

The tiny bundle of nerves brushed one knuckle, and he rubbed at it, reveling in her response. Sliding a digit into her channel, he felt the tightness, ready for him with slick lubrication.

"Addie, I'm going to slide in, fill you up. Make you scream my name, but I'll capture it with my mouth. We'll be one. Complete."

He worked her now with determined sweeps until the rapid breathing, the glow of her skin warned him she was peaking. A second finger joined the first. He pumped and urged, murmured until she splintered, body arching up off the floor.

⁂

Never before had Addie experienced anything like the orgasm that screamed through her at Jack's ministrations.

Her body felt like a finely tuned violin. His fingers the bow that played her until the final note, her cry of pleasure, died away.

Now, here she lay, body exposed and him still half dressed, smiling at her and licking the evidence of her orgasm from his fingers. *God. So fucking hot!* "Jack?"

He leaned over and kissed her again, tongue sweeping deep, and she tasted herself on him. When he tugged away, his hands were working at the belt, every movement a jerk, his body shaking while moonlight played over his muscular form.

With quaking hands, she brushed his fumbling aside. "Let me." She pulled the buckle, the belt sliding free. Their gaze connected and held for a long second as she popped the button then drew down the zip with a rasp that filled the silence.

His fingers hooked in the waistband and pushed down his jeans and underwear. The length of his erection bobbed, free from the constraints. It was engorged. Ready.

"Jack? Fill me now."

God knew in those few moments, the post-orgasm lethargy fled, her body re-invigorated, ready for him.

She wanted to touch, caress and taste but now hunger roared deep inside, like an empty well screaming to be filled.

Jack's hand quested into a pocket before he shucked the clothing from around his ankles. She heard them drop but didn't care. Tomorrow they would deal with the mess, tonight was for loving.

He bit the corner of the foil pack, and it tore. The condom was rolled on with a quick efficient move before he positioned himself. "I wish I could take more time, but I'll explode soon. I want to be inside you," he growled, and she smiled.

"By all means, lover. Fill me up."

Her legs wound around his waist and with a single surging move he seated himself fully within her and the dance began in earnest. Their hands caught.

"Addie," he muttered. "Wet and hot. So fucking ready for me. All mine."

She moved and writhed, lost in pleasure again. Felt every inch as he leaned forward and flicked the tip of her breast with his tongue before settling his mouth.

Ecstasy was looming, the knot inside her loosening. "Please Jack. Please," she chanted, thighs rhythmically clenching.

Then the maelstrom released, her body like glass, shattered into a million tiny pieces. Reality only a dim memory.

She heard his grunt as she cried out his name, then his lips settled on hers and Jack stiffened, fingers digging deep into her flesh, holding her still.

He woke from the doze he'd dropped into after the lovemaking with Addie had plowed through him.

She wasn't there. The pillows were still warm, and she sat in the armchair, one baby settled at her breast. Naked.

Now he allowed his gaze to take in the sight she shared.

Seriously hot.

Their gazes met over the feeding baby. "Fiona was fussing. I didn't want her to wake Leanne."

"Does it hurt?" While he waited for her to answer he searched for something to cover his genitals. There was no way he'd scar the baby with the sight of his nakedness.

"No, and what are you doing? I was enjoying the view." She smiled, a glint in her eyes.

"I'm naked. She's a tiny baby and doesn't need to see her Daddy like this."

Her smiled broadened. "Daddy, huh? I think you're safe, *Daddy*. She's busy feeding, and it's not like she'll remember. But next time I feed them at night, we'll be in bed, and you can cover yourself up if you're embarrassed."

Jack heard the teasing tone in her voice. "You're sure?"

Addie nodded. "What do you think they've been doing for millennia?"

He grunted. The baby released the breast, and she slid the little girl to her shoulder until a gentle burp erupted. "Is there a doctor on the island?"

His guts chilled. "She's sick?"

"No. But she will need to see someone, to make sure her vaccinations in order and Leanne's too. They're okay now, while I'm breast feeding but that will only last while it's their only source of food."

The terror that had settled in his chest evaporated. "Uh, there's a nurse. The one you first saw. We can ask her." Was this the reality of all fathers? This cold lump settling in his chest at the thought they might be ill and require medical assistance? Were the facilities here enough to sustain them if they were truly ill?

"Are you okay, Jack? Is something wrong?"

He looked at her, shook his head then stopped the action. Love, the kind he felt now towards the girls and Addie meant he must be honest. "No. It just occurred to me we don't have a trained doctor on the island. I... We need one. To keep everyone safe. More than one, if we can track some down."

She opened her mouth, and he thought she would say something before she rose with the baby and retreated to the bedroom.

He waited, and she returned, knelt before him still gloriously naked. The moonlight filtered through the windows. "Jack, you can't do everything." Her hand cupped his cheek. "You're plugging holes all over the place but at some point, someone will get sick. They'll die, whether there's a doctor here or not."

Covering her hand with his, the responsibility weighed heavily. "I know, but it doesn't feel like enough."

He rose and padded to the kitchen, withdrawing the champagne from the freezer before it settled like ice and slid it into the fridge. Not tonight, he told himself. Soon. But not now.

Re-entering the lounge, he removed the needle from the record and reached for her hand. "Your room or mine?"

She grimaced. "Mine. We need to be near the babies."

He gave a nod, wound his arm around her midsection and together they retreated to the bedroom, but not before he determined as the babies got older, they'd have their own room. Parents needed their space, after all.

CHAPTER 11

*A*ddie was up early, the babies waking before Jack stirred and she took the time to carry them to the lounge. Once they were changed and fed, she rattled about in the kitchen. *There's certainly something about waking in a man's arms,* she thought with a smile. *Especially Jack's.*

The kettle boiled as he ambled into the room. His gaze taking in the toast she'd made, the coffee she poured.

"Everything okay?"

She noted the careful distance he kept and frowned. "On my side, yes. How about yours?"

The tension she'd felt radiating from him melted. He stepped up, took her in his arms and kissed her. Long and leisurely. "You were gone when I woke," he murmured against her lips. "I didn't want to crowd you if you'd had... second thoughts."

She didn't miss the uncertainty in his voice. "Never."

"Good. Because I don't want to lose you. I feel...:" he rubbed his chest, and a pink tinge colored his cheeks. "Dammit, I love you, Addie. You and those girls. I want to you to stay with me. As my wife."

Her eyes opened wide. Truth inserted itself into her brain. "I... That's what I want too." Any concerns she had weren't important because what she felt was strong and deep. As if those emotions had rooted down from the first time she'd seen him and grown, shooting out in order to establish itself. "I love you too, Jack. You're going to be the world's best Daddy to Leanne and Fiona. And any other children we have."

His eyes glinted. "Good. That's settled. We should eat."

Knowing how the male mind worked, she couldn't hide the smile. Emotional discussions weren't usually high on a guy's list of things to do, and once complete, they usually needed to change the subject.

Once breakfast was cleared the two of them collected the babies and headed for the office. She, to finalize the lists he'd managed to acquire from most of the regional coordinators, along with a promise that the young woman replacing Carl would meet with her on Saturday.

Instead of heading directly for his office, Jack headed to the library, and she wondered if he was looking for stuff on the Tasman Bridge, then shrugged. He was the engineer after all, and only he could determine what they needed.

⁂

*J*ack paced. "We need a boat. Something big." The old shipping channel logs were lying around somewhere. True, not many large craft sailed between the island and the mainland, but there were regular cargo ships that moored off the coast nearby, when the weather was rough. Maybe there was something he could use?

He also wracked his brain thinking about the concerns he'd raised with Addie. There were young people all over the island. Fertile, though no pregnancies he knew of. The midwife was more than capable of the run-of-the-mill he guessed. But what if something went wrong? What if they needed advanced care? There wasn't anyone on hand, the ambulance driver was dead, along with others who'd made their life safer.

"The midwife might know of someone." If they're still alive, dickhead. "We need her to make a list. See if we can get a doctor or two here. Offer a home for them and any family members." It meant more mouths to feed, but they could make it work. So long as they carefully used the resources available.

The radio operator, they'd learned, lived on the far side of the island, he might be able to scare someone up to contact the people the midwife listed. If necessary, he'd cobble together a team. Send them out to wherever they might be. Find and retrieve the targets and bring them to safety.

He scribbled down notes of his thoughts. He needed to go see Thomas too. Check in with the bridge crew and make sure things were okay, and of course, see what Carl was doing. He didn't trust the old man one whit. He'd be either white anting or planning insurrection. Neither would be an assist.

Stalking down the hall he caught sight of Addie hard at work. "I have to go out. I've got to see some people. You okay here?"

"Yeah. Jack?"

He raised an eyebrow as she was up and out of her chair, sliding toward him with her graceful stride. The kiss was soft. "Be safe."

Catching her hand, Jack caressed her cheek. "Stay inside and I'll be back as soon as I can. I'll be gone a while, though."

She nodded, and he turned on his heel and headed for the door, satisfied only when he saw it locked. After yesterday, he'd not be taking any chances with Addie or the girls safety.

Before he started the car, he touched the button of the walkie talkie. "Yeah?"

"Tom. You free for a while?"

A long pause. "Yes, sure. What's up?"

"I'll explain in the car." He cut the connection and started the car, glancing at the petrol indicator. He'd need to fuel up soon. The police had set up gates and CCTV around the fuel bowsers, agreeing that keeping the usage to as few as possible and only for those who needed it, would help it last until they could source alternative transport. "Something else to add to the list." A plan was forming. Dangerous, yet infinitely important if the island community was to survive.

Thomas waited on the corner outside the station and climbed into the vehicle then they sped off. "I need to check on the bridge crew first. But I've an idea. We need doctors, some extra supplies. Ways to get around the island that don't rely on cars. More seeds according to the gardening crew and things like sprayers and fertilizer—"

"And hello to you too, Jack, my friend."

Ignoring Thomas' sarcasm, Jack thrust a pencil and notepad he'd taken to keeping in the car door for notes. "Write that down first. We need a scouting expedition. We also need a boat. Something big and with speed. Something to drive into the bridge."

"What?" Thomas bellowed the word and Jack winced. "What the fuck are you thinking?"

"Actually, it was Addie. She borrowed a book from the library."

"A fictional story isn't going to solve our problem, Jack. Your girl-friend should—"

He growled. "Just shut up and listen. It's a history book of Tasmania. She showed me pictures from the Tasman Bridge disaster. The *Illawarra* hit the bridge, collapsing a section in the night. Hit the pylons and down it came."

Thomas jerked beside him. "You're thinking of... Won't that sink the boat?"

Jack gave a nod. "More than likely. We need to work out the exact co-ordinates, set the autopilot and get off before it hits. But we need a big boat, like a large pleasure vessel, something with speed and agility or a Ro-Ro. We need force to do the job for us."

"A Ro-Ro?"

"Ro-Ro. Roll on Roll off vessel."

"What exactly are you thinking?"

"Lee's boat might work. He invested in one of those experimental remote coupling systems. We get a barge and hook it up."

Thomas was staring at him, like he was mad, but his brain whirred with thoughts of how it would work. "I know it will need time to build up speed, but we can do it gently right? Take it three or four nautical miles out. More, if necessary, since this isn't my thing, I don't know for sure how far. Or will we need something bigger, like to Ro-Ro you mentioned. Whatever we do, we need an experienced seaman for this bit. Depending on the size of the boat, it tugs the barge as it goes under the bridge and using the remote coupling releases the barge. So long as whoever is off the boat, it won't matter if the system doesn't work. Not really."

"Then why choose a boat like that?"

"Because we can use it for fishing in the ocean. We don't want to waste any equipment if we have an option. We drive the vessel into the pylons, and it buckles. The weight and twist do the rest of the task for us."

"Fuck me," whispered Thomas.

"No thanks." Jack laughed and Thomas grunted.

"You think it'll work?"

Jack's mirth dried up. "It's all we have. But there's just one small hitch." He inhaled, because this was part of the scouting party plan. "We need a vessel large enough. There's none here on the island. We need to get to the mainland, take a crew. While there, we gather supplies, anyone in need of evac and move with speed. We need to track down a doctor or two, this is our best opportunity, Thomas."

They pulled up at the end of the bridge and Jack maneuvered the car ready for their return.

Climbing out, he glanced at the gate. It was holding but by the looks of the buckled metal, he knew time was drawing short.

Gus, the man currently on duty along with three friends exited the large, reinforced tower they'd erected hastily. "Hey, Jack. Thomas. Come to inspect?"

"Yeah. How're things?"

Gus shook his head, his salt and pepper hair standing upright. "Days are still okay, but the nights are getting hairy. We need a long-term plan to protect the island and this one won't cut it for too much longer."

"When did they damage the gate?" He nodded to the bends.

"Two days ago. They heard music and sounds of movement.

Yesterday, they had another good go at it. There were noises, I thought like screams in the afternoon, that had them all excited."

Jack's lip curled. That would have been Sarah and Addie. Clearly, they'd captured more attention than anyone would have hoped for. "I'm working on a plan, Gus. I need a day or two to confirm then a few more to plan. Can you keep them at bay that long?"

"I'll do my best, Jack. But we can't hold them too much longer. Every night there's more. And they're hungrier. It's like they're starving."

He couldn't miss the intensity of the man's stare. "Anything else you need?"

Gus shook his head, and they made their farewells before heading back to the island.

"Things are going to get worse before they improve," Thomas murmured. "But your plan is the only one I've heard so far that could work. We need to go with it. Let me talk to the Sarge. We'll call a meeting day after tomorrow."

Jack nodded his agreement. "Now to Carl, he's a problem and I need to check in on him. Plus catch the midwife and the radio operator."

CHAPTER 12

Jack had a job to do, but when he told her he'd be heading to the mainland soon on a mission, Addie's heart lodged firmly in her throat while the emotions tore at her. "Are..." she had to clear her throat because it suddenly turned hoarse. "Are both you and Thomas going?"

Jack nodded his head. "The Sarge will have to be more on the ground, and he's training recruits right now. They'll patrol day and night, in an old security car we found."

"What if it goes wrong?"

"Oh, Addie. I know you're frightened; I am too. We rounded up the Catholic Priest, and he's going to marry us before I go. I want you to have my name. That way the house and everything is yours. I'd adopt the babies too, but we haven't talked about it." His arms came around her, and she wanted to cry, but held it in.

"It's not... the house, Jack. I lost Darcy, and that was bad enough, but losing you? I think that will crush me." She looked up, knowing her face was red, her eyes swollen and her nose a shiny mess. "I know I have to be strong, but I don't think..." she shook her head.

"Addie, I have to go. You know that don't you?"

She nodded feeling worse because she did. "Yeah."

"I promise to take every precaution. I'll be careful because my wife will be waiting for me. The one I intend to make more babies with. The one I will grow old with. Because I love you, I will be super cautious."

"God, I'm sorry. I know you have to go, and I need to be grown-up and strong. I will be by the time you go, but I just want you to know... I won't lie to you, Jack." Her fingers clutched at his shirt, he sighed, and he held her close. "What I'm feeling right now? This is me. My honest emotions."

"I know." He whispered against her hair. "I don't want to go, but it's necessary, Addie. Tomorrow we will marry, while our radio operator is trying to get a message through to the doctors Sheila listed. Since I don't suppose you ever got over to her with everything that happened, we'll do that too."

She nodded and swiped at her face, laughing when he shoved a handkerchief into her hands. "I'm sorry. I will be strong while you're gone. I promise."

"Come on. We should go home. Take an early mark. We can start fresh the day after tomorrow, or the day after that."

Addie bit her lip, feeling even more like a sappy idiot. She'd just blubbered all over him, then he'd offered her a marriage—albeit without a gown—and even suggested an extra day afterwards. He was an important person in the community, if somewhat removed.

"Is there anyone you want to ask?"

He started to shake his head then stopped. "Actually, there is. Kelly."

Her mind spun sluggishly for a second then the blonde woman's face came to her. "The woman who brought the fish?"

"She and Thomas were together while at school. Just before we graduated something happened, and they broke up. Kelly hasn't really moved on. I don't think. And Thomas? He's reserved with women. They..." Jack shrugged. "It's going to sound stupid," he warned. "They feel like they belong together, yet neither will meet the other on neutral ground. If Kelly knows Thomas is at an event, she won't go. He won't go where she's headlining with her singing either. But I'd like them both there."

"Well, then they should come," Addie croaked.

"Actually," and now Jack smiled. "She is good at finding stuff and the little wedding store here on the island has been locked up, though I'm sure we could arrange something perfect for you."

Addie's mouth opened and shut. With Darcy they'd done cocktail outfits in front of the judge. To be able to have a wedding gown...

"We can stop by, see if she and her dad are at the house. Then we could all go to the shop—"

Now that she was starting to find her equilibrium, Addie shook her head. "No way. If I'm having a wedding gown, you aren't coming for the choosing and fitting."

Jack's mouth flattened. "No fucking way, Addie. I'll sit outside, if necessary, but there's no way you and our babies are going into that store unprotected. Got it?"

She wondered for a moment if he realized what he'd said and grinned. But the furrowed brow told her she'd best put his mind at rest before pointing that out. "Okay, you sit in the car. The babies come with me, given they're due soon for a feed. Does Kelly have a car?"

He blinked rapidly. "Yes."

"Then she can take the gown with her and tomorrow she can come by with it. Maybe she'll help me dress and assist with the babies."

"And what about—"

"You'll be making yourself scarce until the wedding. Kelly might even drive me."

"Huh," he grunted. "I was thinking we might have the ceremony on the beach. In front of the house."

"Even better. You can fish for our supper before you dress. Now, let's go, my soon-to-be-husband."

Outside the shop, Jack tapped the steering wheel. Sitting here wasn't his plan at all, but Addie wanted some of the trappings of a wedding. Hell, she more than deserved it. He'd hang the moon for her if she asked. Not that she had.

His walkie talkie squawked. "Thomas?"

"Yeah. Where are you?"

Jack rattled off the name of the store and Thomas swore, "What the Fuck are you doing there?"

"Addie's inside getting a dress for tomorrow, Thomas. And you will be there, won't you? You are, after all my best man."

"Yeah, I'll be there. But we need to talk, can you get away?"

"Not exactly, but you can come here."

Thomas swore and agreed, stated he'd be there in ten minutes and Jack frowned. If Thomas was on the blower this quickly then something had happened. Good or bad, either way, he refused to let anything ruin tomorrow.

He watched and soon enough the car showed in the rear-view mirror. Thomas climbed out, and Jack met him by the rear of the car.

"Whose car is that?" He nodded to the little sedan parked in front of him.

"A friend's car. Inside helping Addie choose a dress for her and the girls."

Thomas narrowed his eyes. "Kelly? She's involved?"

'Damn it, Tom. One day. You can practice civility for a single day. For me. For Addie."

Thomas' eyes were icy cold. "Whatever," he snarled. "Nathan found us the doctors Sheila suggested. A couple. He's emergency, and she's an anesthesiologist. Older, but their daughter is also a doctor, married with two little kids. Husband is dead. The other sister was compromised too. They want to come to the island. The grandkids are terrified and from what I heard they saw the attack on their father. For the sake of the kids, they holed up on the family property, but when they got news, the kids heard. The family wants to join us,

Jack. There' are a couple of other medicals hunkering down with them."

Jack scratched his head, wondering at their luck. "How did the word get to them so quickly?"

Thomas bared his teeth. "There's a single policeman there. He's been keeping an eye on them, as they refused to move into the reinforced town area. Slowly, their populace has deteriorated. Then the residents started committing suicide, and there's only five or six left. They want to join the doctors; come to the island."

"We've plenty of room. How did we go finding a large enough vessel?"

Thomas grinned. "The Pride of McErin was in port—right at the edge of the Marcoorella marina. Still there. She's got a barge in tow because they were going to retrofit it as a dredge. The boat alone is big enough that we can fit our passengers. Even better, she was carrying grocery items. Wheat, flour, and so on. The barge was being transported to Brisbane but when they closed the port, everything was halted. There's also a couple of other vessels that would be useful to us."

"Then, we focus on the Pride of McErin first."

"Hearing you. We also need to know what else we need that they may be able to supply."

Jack shook his head. "Sheila would know. We should check in with her. Can you make contact?"

Thomas nodded. "Sure, we can go see her in the morning."

"No go, Tom. I promised my bride tomorrow. No work."

"You're shitting me, right?" Thomas' eyes bugged out.

"Nope. Not at all." Now Jack gave a smile. "Think of it this way, at least we all get a day's break."

"Like the zombies will too," Thomas added.

Too true, but they can only hope for a little break in the day-on-day-off grind.

*A*ddie woke to an empty spot in the bed beside her. An envelope was propped against the pillow. She reached out, fingers shaking with trepidation.

Darling Addie,

I can't wait to see you this afternoon. Kelly will be by soon with your gown, and whatever else you women do in preparation. Take the time to enjoy her company, because tonight, you're all mine.

I'll see you by the small pier at one.

With all my love

Jack

Tears sprang, burning the lids of her eyes. "Oh Jack!" One hot tear tracked down her cheek as she traced his name.

So much. So quick. She regretted nothing, because her heart was full. Fiona and Leanne and now Jack. Life might be difficult in this new reality. Nothing promised of a long future with the threat of the zombies, but for her right now came pretty damned close to amazing. *If you discount his dangerous mission to come,* whispered her brain.

"Stop it!"

She rose, attending to her needs then those of the babies who woke and as she headed for the kitchen to make a coffee a knock sounded. "Addie? Addie?"

Marching to the top of the stairs, she peered over and there waiting was Kelly. "Come on up." At the top of the stairs, Kelly gave her a quick hug. "Coffee?"

"Oh, you're a darling. A quick one before we begin." Kelly slid the white bag onto the lounge. "I'll just run downstairs and grab the rest of the stuff I brought with me."

Addie wasn't sure what other stuff there could be but headed for the kitchen, filling the kettle with water. She'd placed it on the counter-top and flicked the switch when Kelly entered the room. "I love this place. I've only visited a few times, when Tom and I..."

"When you and Tom...?" Addie waited for Kelly to explain, but she didn't, and Addie wondered about that.

"Where are those gorgeous babies? I found the most marvelous baby dresses after you left yesterday. There were a couple of options, so I grabbed them in three sizes, just to be sure."

Surprised and feeling a little bit out of control, Addie nodded. "Sure."

The kettle boiled, and she took a second, while filling the cups to let her mind refocus. "Jack said he'd meet us at one."

"He did?" asked Kelly. "What about it being bad luck to see the bride before the wedding?"

Unable to control the smile, Addie handed Kelly her cup. "Well, he left a letter for me." She pinked, the heat scorching her cheeks and Kelly quirked a brow without saying a word.

"Let's go sit in the lounge. We have a little while before the girls wake and it would be good to have a shower, but I need this drink."

Settling on the chairs she waited, hoping Kelly would break the sudden silence that stretched.

"I've known Jack a long time. He's a good man. He also loves you, that much is clear. When he sent me over with the fish, he smiled. It was deep and his eyes shone. Even with Sarah—"

"She was the woman he..." The words stuck in Addie's throat.

"Oh, she was a money-grubbing bitch. Saw the house, the nice car and thought she was on a winner. Best thing Tom ever did was tell him about the hag." Kelly's eyes narrowed. "What I'm trying to say is Jack's a great guy. He's honest and hardworking. He's already bowled over by your two. He's the kind of guy woman would run after, but he's never really been a grand gestures man. Until you."

The words wound around Addie. "You're telling me if I hurt him...?"

Kelly's eyes widened. "Oh! Oh, no! I don't think you would. I'm pretty good at sizing people up and I've watched you talking about him. The house is immaculate. The babies adorable and you've captured something inside him. I just wanted to say, if you have any questions about his honesty, don't."

Addie released the muscles she didn't even know had tensed. "I... I love him, Kelly. That's the long and short of it. I wouldn't commit if I wasn't totally sure of him and how he bonded with the babies, though. I'm so blessed though, because he's protective of them. He loves them already. I can't miss the bond they've already got with him. I'm..." She rubbed at burning eyes. "I'm lucky to have found him."

"You both are."

The quiet tones of Kelly's words tugged at Addie. "Thomas hurt you?"

Kelly shrugged. "Yes. No. We hurt each other."

"It's not too late. You're both alive and—"

This time, when Kelly shook her head, it was slow, laced with regret. "It is. It was always going to be from the moment we both walked away." She gulped, like it was an effort to swallow her sadness, and forced a smile, but it didn't reach her eyes. "Now, you should shower, then we can get started." Kelly drank deeply of her coffee, and Addie knew the conversation about Kelly and Thomas was done.

Once she'd finished her drink, Kelly grabbed the cups, waving Addie off to the shower.

A quick wash of the hair, then she cleansed her skin. "Best I can do," she whispered with a grimace.

The babies started to wail just as Addie completed brushing her teeth and she entered the bedroom, before stopping and staring. Kelly had been busy, hanging up the gown, laying out underwear too, so filmy it would do little more than lightly contain her assets. She had had also laid the pretty baby dresses on the bed.

"Oh good. You should feed them, then change into your bridal lingerie."

"But..." Addie blushed. "I mean..."

Kelly laughed. "You only get married once or maybe twice. Jack was adamant, you were to get the full treatment. So come on, get settled."

Quickly gathering everything together, Kelly blushed. "Umm do you want some privacy?"

The question startled Addie, but then she smiled. "No. Stay and talk to me. Show me the baby dresses." With the feeding pillow on her lap and a pillow at her back, she settled the two babies in position before releasing the clips of her nursing bra.

"Umm is that bra necessary? I mean, do you need to wear that one?"

"What? Oh no, it's just easier, but so long as I give them a feed before, they'll be fine, and I can wear a normal bra. And it's really pretty. Just, there's not much of it." It was a white lacy balcony confection with a deep 'V' and scalloped edges, an intricate vine and flower pattern which curled around where her nipples would sit. The material fine and see through. The matching thong left little to the imagination.

"I..." Now it was Addie's turn to gulp. "Those panties won't cover much."

"They're not meant to," added Kelly with a smile. "Tonight's your wedding night. Time to howl and all that."

"Oh," she murmured. "Yes."

Time passed slowly for Jack while awaiting one o'clock. He'd fished with Thomas then set up chairs for those who'd gather for the ceremony on the beach. Thomas' mother would attend and take photos for posterity, while the Sargent would leave his office at the police station, something he rarely did since the outbreak. Kelly would attend with her father and the Catholic Priest would conduct the ceremony. He wasn't sure if Addie was religious, but in these trying times it seemed best to hedge his bets.

It was a lovely mid-Autumn day. The sea breeze blew softly, the palm trees swayed gently, dotting the edges of the beach. The sky shone a pale blue, and it was one of those photo-perfect days, he thought.

Nerves assailed him, as he readjusted the good white pants, he'd rolled up slightly in deference to the sand, and blue shirt. He'd opted for barefoot and wondered if Addie would too.

"She'll be here soon enough, Jack," the priest offered.

"Yeah. I know." But it didn't calm the thrashing butterflies filling his stomach.

He heard them before he looked. Two little gurgling babies and his mind blanked.

She was moving toward him, gracefully making her way along the beach, on Kelly's dad's arm. She carried one baby and Kelly, dressed in a seafoam green dress, carried the other.

The vision in white stole his breath. He scanned her, the loose white dress flowing around her body. Chiffon, his mind offered. With cut-outs at the shoulder and a high waist which accentuated her beauty, so she appeared like a young Madonna. Her titian locks framing her face with a riot of tiny curls.

Jack reached for her hand, noted that it shook. "Okay?"

She smiled and nodded. "Yeah."

They turned and faced the priest and he spoke the words of love that bound them together. When it was done, he leaned forward and kissed her, keeping it light, because if he didn't, he wasn't sure he'd stop. His body tight and wired, it had been aware of her presence beside him during the ceremony. The way her breasts rose and feel beneath the light material.

The people gathered congratulated them and all he could think of was 'go away. I want to be alone with my bride.' Instead, he controlled it. Took Fiona in his arms while Addie held Leanne and posed for a photo.

"There now, a beautiful family portrait. When things get back to normal, you'll have it framed and hung on the wall," Thomas' mother enthused.

While Jack wasn't sure that day would ever come, for all their sakes he hoped he was wrong.

CHAPTER 13

Addie settled the girls in Jack's old room. Thomas had managed to scare them up a cot each and while she had concerns about putting them each on their own, Jack had suggested they push the cots side by side, so Leanne and Fiona could still see each other.

Apparently, this was Thomas' gift to them on their wedding day.

Jack touched her shoulder. "They're both out like lights."

"I know." But she stayed a moment longer, aware that she needed to leave them, but never had they spent a night out of the same room as she occupied. Another quick glance at the monitor on the change table—Kelly had found and added to the babies' room —had Addie sighing.

"They'd be fine."

"I know Jack. It's just, they've shared a room with me since they were born. I feel like I'm being torn."

"You want them back in our room? If that's what you need, we'll—"

"No, Jack. They need their space, and we need ours. I just feel odd about it."

"Addie— "

She laid a finger against his mouth. "It's our wedding night, Jack." She took one step then another away from the doorway, her hand taking his and dragging him toward the lounge.

They'd eaten on the beach, fish and salad, freshly picked by Thomas' mother from her greenhouse. After the guests left, they found baskets of fruit and delicious items on the steps, gifts from those he worked with on the island.

"You had champagne ready, and we didn't drink it. Kelly nearly opened it this morning, but I fended her off valiantly!"

Jack laughed. "Kelly likes to celebrate a little too much. But we will share the bottle, enjoy some of the goodies and dance."

Addie hoped that wasn't all they'd do but kept silent. She'd fed the babies quietly while Jack was busy collecting the gifts and ensuring the place was locked up tight. When he'd gone to enter, she'd asked him to wait. Knew that it surprised him. He hadn't yet seen what she wore under the gown. Once more she smiled. The fastener was a simple hook and eye with a zip on the side, hidden from view so she was able to remove it long enough to attend to the babies' needs and slide it back on afterwards.

Now she noted the way he'd laid out the lounge. Piles of pillows made a bed, a soft looking throw rug sat on the lounge and the room was lit by candlelight.

"Oh, Jack," she breathed.

"I don't have a gift for you, my love."

She teared up. "Neither do I."

"Your gift was you and our beautiful babies." The words echoed inside her, filling Addie up with a warm glow.

Reaching up, she curled her hands into Jacks hair and pulled him close. "I love you, Jack. I love that you're my husband and the Daddy of our girls. I will do everything I can to make you happy."

He kissed her with a swift glance. "I know. Addie, I want forever with you. I want to make babies and live a life of laughter. I want to get old and have you complain because of dirty underwear and the bad dad jokes as we watch the world go by. All I want is you by my side. Forever."

Stepping away he poured two glasses of champagne after releasing the cork with a loud pop.

Addie laughed, then their gazes met. Drinking in the sight of each other.

The oxygen in her lungs fled, and he reached for her glass, slid it onto the table and moved to the center of the room. He pressed a button on the remote from his pocket, and the sound of a voice filled the air, smooth and seductive. "Addie," he murmured and held out his hand.

She went into his embrace, loving the strength of her husband, her body already on fire with arousal and she felt the jump of a nerve in her neck.

"Dance with me," his words erotic and hungry.

Tugging her close, she sighed as the outline of his body moved against hers. Her breasts peaked beneath the lace constraining her breasts, the lace between her legs growing damp as she felt the outline of his erection hidden by his pants.

Jack's hands made circles on her back, and fire streaked through her. "Jack," she murmured. "I want you."

He smiled, and she looked up, his eyes hooded, the hint of arousal cresting his cheeks with a pale blush. "And I want you, Addie. I want to see you. All of you."

With a smile, Addie danced back slowly and lifted her hand, unhooked the hidden eye and released the zip.

Jack removed his shirt, and the sight of his chest, bare and illuminated by candlelight dried her mouth. "You're beautiful, Jack."

His hands played with his belt, and she slid the dress to the floor, scooped it up and deposited it on the lounge while he looked down, unfastening and cursing his pants. She laughed, and he looked up.

Jack's eyes narrowed, zeroing in on her.

Her nipples puckered beneath the lace.

"That ought to be illegal," he hoarsely muttered. His pants fell with a whisper to the floor. His arousal jutting proudly before him.

"You like it?"

His step was uneven, and he reached, tracing the whorl covering her breast. "The vein surrounds your nipple, making it look like a ripe grape. Ready for me to feast upon. Those panties... Are they wet yet, Addie? Are you hot and ready for me?"

She almost swallowed her tongue at the dark words he whispered against her mouth, before he claimed her lips in a scorching kiss.

He tasted of champagne and hunger. His body crowding hers, and she slid her hands over his shoulders.

"I'm so hot, I could melt."

He shuddered, the movement against her sensitized breasts had her gasping.

His hand slid down between them, cupping a breast and flicking against her nipple. Addie cried out and arched, while lightning arced through her body, her sex quivered and tensed. "Jack," she moaned.

The hand that bedeviled continued its exploration as he moved his mouth to her neck. "You're so damned sexy. I want to explode inside you, Addie. To feel all of you."

Fingers found the band of the lacy thong and caressed over the pattern. "I could see you through the panties before. Nothing is hidden beneath that covering."

His fingers moved between her legs, and he stilled, his body tensing. "Jesus, you're hot and wet. Drenched. Feel what you do to me."

Her body shook with tremors as hunger roared deep inside. He guided her hand to cup his erection. "Oh God, Jack, I want you inside me."

"Soon," he crooned, his hand questing beneath the lace. Sliding between the folds hiding her overheated core. "Feel my touch, the way I slide and rub. Every touch an act of love."

She released him and her hands pushed at her panties while he laughed softly. "I need you, Jack. I need you now. Inside me."

Their gazes met and held.

Their mouths crashed together, the storm growing inside her. Only he could soothe the raggedness and she rolled the panties off, down over her hips and let them hit the floor between her legs.

Jack devoured her, opened mouthed kisses that trailed down her body, found her breasts and covered the tips. She arched and raised her leg.

He grabbed it, slid it around his waist then his hands found the roundness of her ass. Lifted her and she was impaled, his hard cock buried deep inside her that she rode. Needing the release only Jack could give.

They grunted and gyrated, bodies jerking together as their passion filled the air with a musky scent.

Addie shattered in his arms, and his fingers dug deep into the flesh of her hips as he came, jetting deeply.

A second passed. Then another.

Bonelessly, she slid to the floor and his hands steadied her. "Oh... wow." She whispered and Jack slid his forehead against hers. Their bodies still working hard in the aftermath of the wild explosion.

"Yeah. Something like that." He took her hand and laid her down on the pillows, his hand sliding over the band he'd slid on her finger earlier in the day. "My mother would be proud to have you wear that."

She glanced down, then back up. "This was hers?"

He swallowed deeply, then sighed. "It was. I retrieved it just before..." He kissed her, a soft and gentle slide of mouths. "She'd have loved you. So would Dad."

He lay down and scooped her close into his arms. "Just as I do."

CHAPTER 14

ack rose, his gaze taking in his wife's face. "Wife," he whispered to himself and stepped into the shower. Water sluiced over his skin, and he hurried through the mundane daily acts, shaving and combing down his hair.

Then he dragged on loose pajama bottoms and headed for the kitchen. In his mind, coffee and a breakfast of fruit in bed was the perfect way to start his first day of his new life.

At the other end of the house came a wail. "I'm up," Addie called. For a moment he had a sense that this is what his life would have been like before the virus. Home, family and a good job. His parents —a thickening of his throat had to be cleared. "They'd loved Addie, but no amount of wishing will bring them back." Instead, he'd honor their memory by being the best father he could be.

A knock at the front door had him frowning, and he headed out. Thomas waited, his mouth a thin line. "We have a problem, Jack. Can I come up?"

"Uh, yeah. Just let me tell Addie you're here."

He left Thomas to let himself in and found Addie changing Leanne. "Thomas is here," he nodded at her nakedness. "I'll grab your robe."

She pinked, and he wanted to kiss her, to sink into her softness, but the sound of footsteps and the cupboards in the kitchen brought him back to reality. With quick steps he found the robe on the end of the bed, his hands tensing as memories from the night before cascaded, and with a huff he marched back to the nursery.

Addie took it and smiled. "Thanks, I'll be down once I sort these two out."

Jack retreated to the kitchen where Thomas was closing the fridge door. "You're almost out of milk."

"So, what's wrong?"

Thomas tipped his head to the side. "Maybe we should go sit at the table. Addie'll be through soon?"

"When she's done." He scooped up the kettle and poured the two cups for himself and Addie and they stepped into the dining area. "So, what's the problem?"

"There was another attack last night. We don't know where the fucking nest is. And we heard from the mainland that hings are getting worse and our doctors need to get out now."

Jack rubbed his forehead. This wasn't the news he was hoping for. "How soon is now?"

"We should leave either today or tomorrow. There's talk of guerrillas roaming the streets on the coast and even down south. We got news of settlements being established and attacked. Some are strong and survivors. Others aren't so lucky. This lot are in danger and if we don't get them soon…"

Thomas didn't need to say any more, because Jack could see it in his mind's eye. "What kind of transport is organized?"

"There's a truck or two. I think also a car. We're going to have to move people quickly and I recommend not travelling on the bridge. Last night's incursion was the worst so far. Gus and his crew are asking for reinforcements. We just don't have any."

"The gates?"

"Held but are damaged after last night. I've suggested we look at how we can shore it up, but we aren't going to be able to hold them off much longer. If they get over the bridge and meet up with the nest, that's here…"

The memory of his father, the evil glint and the noises had Jack's gut churning. "Fuck!"

"Yeah. Jack, we need decisions made. Now."

Addie stepped into the room several minutes later, clad in jeans and t-shirt, her red hair caught back in a ponytail. "Thanks for the coffee." She scooped it up.

He turned to her, and she must have read something on his face. "What's wrong?"

"I need to go to the mainland. Tonight." Jack watched as her face paled, and her eyes widened.

"Tonight?"

He nodded and held out a hand. "Things are desperate. We have to demolish that section of bridge before it's too late, Addie. I've tracked down a vessel capable, and some much-needed supplies. But we need to go today. I need to put together my team and equipment."

She gulped and though he read fear in her eyes, she nodded. "I understand."

The knot of tension in his gut eased a little. He didn't want to go, but the responsibility was his.

Thomas cleared his throat. "I'll arrange for them to meet you at the office, then. In an hour?"

Jack nodded and Thomas rose with a 'thanks for the coffee,' and left.

Addie watched him. "You need to go into the office?"

"We need to plan and get supplies."

"Then I'll come with you." She rose, and he stared.

"You can't come with me to the mainland."

Her smile was slight and didn't reach her eyes. "Not the mainland, the office. I'll help you with getting the supplies together. Get everything into backpacks so your arms are free. Maybe Kelly can come stay with the babies for a few hours."

Jack reached out and tugged her close. He knew she was fighting her emotions. *God knows, she's stronger than me.* "I love you, Addie. Don't you forget that."

"I won't Jack. Never."

Kelly arrived quickly after the message was sent out and Jack and Addie climbed into the car. "Jack? You'll be safe, won't you?" God, Addie hated that tiny quaver in her voice, but controlling it was nigh on impossible.

Her gut twisted every time she considered the danger he'd be facing.

They arrived at the office, and he gripped her hand tight. "I'm coming home to you, Addie. Maybe not tonight, but every night."

Once inside, Jack gave instructions to find backpacks, water bottles, dried foods, in case they had to hide out—and that had her stomach somersaulting. By the time Thomas arrived, she'd made up six packs.

Jack met him at the door and shook the hands of the twelve men who followed Thomas into the building.

"These guys are the best we have. Lucas, Mike and Jeremy are ex-army. Nico and Terry are police, and the other guys are a mix of shooters and miners. They're quick on their feet, with good eyes. If we break into groups of seven on each team, we can get the jobs we need to do, out of the way quickly." Thomas flicked open one pack and glanced at Addie. "Good job."

She knew he still wasn't sure of her, and she understood his reticence after the Sarah saga, as Kelly had termed it, but she needed him to understand, she'd do nothing to endanger Jack's life. "I've also found some extra walkie talkies. I've plugged them in, so they'll be fully charged by the time you head out."

Jack smiled at her, and it warmed the chilled pit inside her belly. He'd dragged a whiteboard from his office, cleaned it off and wrote the names into teams, mixing up the personnel, as he termed it, so they got the best outcome.

On one wall hung a map. "We arrive here, going in via boat. The bridge now is too volatile, and I don't want to open it, in case the zombies get wind and make a concerted attack. We will be met by the group from Marcoorella here." He drew a large blue 'X' "They have arranged transport for us. My team will be looking for transport, medical items, other useful information. I'll have Addie arrange a list for everyone. If we color code it, then we can work in sub-teams of three with a lookout. I want to try this shopping center here," he drew a red circle on the map, "and the one here." Another red circle was added. "There's a bike store here. I hear there's dozens of bikes already put together and more in boxes at the back of the store. We need everything we can lay our hands on."

Thomas stalked around to the other side of the board. "My team will be travelling to the hinterland. Our target is a family living in Eurangalla, who need safe passage. They'll be ready for us and bringing medical kits, further supplies and kids. There are several doctors in the family, and they wish to relocate to the Island." He breathed out. "The kids are traumatized, so we need to be on our game at all times. We don't know how they'll react."

"But the adults are the prime targets?" One of the men asked.

Jack shook his head. "We need them all. They deserve safety, the kind we have here."

The man nodded and the members of the team who'd started muttering, and frowning settled back down.

"The plan is in and out as quickly as possible. We've got supplies in the backpacks Addie put together. Water, purification straws and dried food. Getting to Eurangella should only take a few hours but we don't know what the team will encounter. We need to be back here within four days. The situation with the bridge is perilous and we're leaving with only the bare minimum to protect those on the island, and we still have an active nest. Any longer and..." Jack didn't finish the sentence. He didn't have to, because everyone's face betrayed their understanding of the situation.

Nico sat up. "When do we leave?"

Thomas grunted, "As soon as the planning meeting is done."

*A*ddie photocopied the request lists, found more dried food and packaged them then grabbed maps, flashlights and ropes Jack hadn't asked for, recognizing that being prepared might just save their lives. She added matches she'd found in a cupboard and some medical kits too. "God knows what they'll need."

The activity kept her mind occupied for now. How she'd handle the next few days? Well, that was anyone's call.

Finally, the teams broke up and the satchels she'd prepared were swung over shoulders. The members trooped from the office until it was just Jack and Addie left.

Her eyes burned, and she used the wall for support. "Addie?"

"Yeah, I'm here, Jack."

He entered the room. Held out a hand and she took it, let him draw her close. They kissed, mouths melded together. Desperation laced through her. She knew he had to go, but she feared what might happen.

Finally, he drew away, looped a strand of hair behind her ear, and gazed at her, like he was willing her to take strength from him. "I'll be back, Addie."

She nodded; unsure her voice would remain even.

"I promise. Take care of our family while I'm away. Remember, I'm coming home to you, because nothing will get between us."

Tears burned her eyes. "I love you."

"I love you too Addie. I'll be home in a few days, but for my sake, try and stay at home unless something urgent occurs, okay?"

She nodded, and he turned, headed for the door and she followed him. In the doorway he stilled, glanced back and smiled. Winked. Then walked away, the door swinging shut after him.

CHAPTER 15

Jack crouched under the overhanging awning. The sun's rays were weak, the clouds heavy and not for the first time on this mission, he wanted to scream. The calm weather of the previous week giving way to drizzling showers and heavy cloud cover.

The zombies were out in force, not liking daylight hours, it seemed these conditions were acceptable for them to wander freely.

"I don't like this situation," muttered Nico, and Jack wanted to agree. They were exposed outside the bike shop, the awning battered and bent. Dark brown stains spattered the metal, and he refused to consider what those stains might be.

"We need those bikes. Transport is something we will soon lack given our fuel usage."

"But on a bike, will we be even able to outrun one of the shufflers? I mean, bikes?" Derision coated Nico's voice.

"When we find the nest, it won't be an issue anymore will it? It'll mean we can get workers where they need to be, so stop complaining, Nico."

They'd been two days looking for the supplies on the lists, and while the medical items had been scooped up, along with bedding, clothing, seeds and gardening equipment and some school items, the bikes were the final item they needed to retrieve.

His people had discovered a trove in one of the stores, a baby goods shop, and he'd grabbed items for Fiona and Leanne more than a little aware that Addie had few toys for the babies. The three boxes were stashed on the transport boat, which was moored off the marina now, and beyond the zombies.

He scanned the area again. "We have to get in. Get one of the boys to carefully pop the door."

Yesterday had nearly been their last, as an exuberant member of the team crashed into a door.

"Nearly there!"

Jack held in his frustration as the man ran at it, with a roar.

Looking around he checked to make sure no one was watching. The crash was loud, and Jack winced. "What the fuck?" He muttered.

The man grinned, gave a double thumbs up and headed inside, to come haring out seconds later. "It's a fucking nest, man!"

The moaning sounds emanating from inside curled Jack's gut. "Get ready!" Even as the zombies attempted to emerge, the team struck as one. Cricket bats and golfing irons, they'd discovered, were more efficient in dispatching at close range than guns. They were also quieter.

The sounds of thwacks and bangs were loud, stomach curdling as was the stench of rot that rose from the creatures, but if they missed any, their lives were potentially over.

By the end, they were spattered and sweating, stinking from heat and the discharge from their quarry, but they were unhurt.

"Good thing they're slow and don't think," added Nico.

Jack agreed.

"Let's get those medical items and get out of here." High on the list was medications from the back of the shop. He'd also added formula and baby items, again aware that the island had women of child-bearing age. Cough mixtures and measures and anything else they could carry easily. Loading up the truck took time, but with a man on point, they moved quickly, boxing things up so they could stack them efficiently.

"We need to get this to the ship quickly. Some of these medications will need to be back in the refrigeration as swiftly as possible." He handed them to other men.

The wharf was empty, and they ferried the items to the small boats waiting, then onto the large boat.

He'd heard nothing from Thomas since early morning. Jack worried and paced. The batteries on the walkie talkie unit were getting low, and they'd agreed to make contact at three in the afternoon. A glance at Jack's watch told him that was another hour away.

Glancing toward the island, a mere speck in the distance, he worried about Addie. Was she alright? The babies?

Concern about the bridge and the nest gnawed at him day and night.

The radio squawked. "Thomas checking in early. I've got them loaded up. We'll head out in the morning."

"All quiet your end?" His gut loosened slightly knowing his friend was still alive.

Silence stretched for a long moment. "Sort of. I'll check in once we're moving, Jack."

"Gotcha. Take care."

Nico came striding towards him. "I got goodies for you, Jack. We managed to get into the shop next door to the chemist, the one with the papered windows."

"What did you find?"

"Sporting goods. Bats, balls, racquets. Cross bows."

Jack stumbled as he moved in Nico's direction. "Say what?"

The man grinned. "Bows, Cross Bows and even the odd compound bow and arrows."

"Well, fuck me!" He grinned.

"Uhh, no thanks, man. That's your wife's territory."

Nico nodded. "Go quietly today, Gary. Don't want a repeat of yesterday's mess."

Gary blushed a bright red and nodded. "Yeah, I learned my lesson, alright."

He jiggled the lock. Grunted and reached into his pocket, withdrawing a paperclip.

Jack didn't speak though he was sure his brows rose and his memory stretching to the day before.

The team waited, faces gazing outward, waiting for a sign of the walkers.

"We're in," muttered Nico and they moved, a now if not well oiled, then a comfortable pattern. Those armed with rifles entered first, to check the aisles. "Clear," they called softly, and his men moved into action.

Boxes moved quickly, then someone decided to open the roller door. "Quicker," Nico muttered.

The first truck full, they started to load the second, and Jack grabbed smaller items. The chains, oils and tools, replacement tubes and tires, so they could repair as things broke down.

They finished quickly and were climbing into the trucks when the dirge began again. "Get us out of here," he demanded, and they were rolling just as a crowd of fifteen to twenty rounded the building. Only when they'd left the area long behind did Jack allow his muscles to relax.

"Heh, we're good at this looting business," crowed Nico.

Jack didn't agree even now. He hated just helping himself, but he had people relying on him.

A sound alerted him, and he turned, watching as vehicles screamed into the marina car park. A car, pulling a caravan and followed by two more cars rolled to a stop.

Tom jumped from the car, just as the gates of the marina moved.

The sound of rifles cocking had Jack's mouth drying.

Someone else jumped from the first car, and Jack let out his breath with a whoosh. "Fuck you, Thomas. You were supposed to let us know you were coming."

Tom ambled forth, limping, his clothes stained and torn. Jack's insides froze.

"I'm not bitten, but we ran into a little problem. Got the family, they're hiding in the caravan. Seems someone else heard about them and wanted their services. They tried to grab us, but we got out of there, not before one of the kids got hit with a bullet. We've got some injuries, but this is the best we could do. There's no ambulances left."

Jack scrubbed his hand over his face. "How bad?"

"Doc Neilsen says he needs surgery, but that means we gotta get to the island. Fast."

Jack scanned the boats moored. At the far end he saw a cruiser. Light and probably fast. "Can you get onto that? If we can boost it, that'll get you back to the island faster. I can supervise the last loading up, get the stragglers on the boat. Mike'll come in as soon as I hail him, he's started to ferry a team across to work the boat."

"You should go with them. Addie'll be beside herself," Thomas muttered.

God knew, he wanted nothing more than to go home, but these were his people. He couldn't leave while they remained. "No. Contact her once you've got the doc and kid to the island hospital, tell her I'm not far away." He prayed he wasn't jinxing the plan with his comments, but Thomas nodded.

"Okay," then Thomas rushed to the back of the caravan, swinging open the doors.

His men streamed over surrounding a young girl who was sobbing, and an older couple. "Get them onto Mike's boat once he moors. Thomas is taking the cruiser." He turned to the man who'd broken into the cycle store. "Gary, can you hot-wire it?"

Jack didn't want to consider how Gary had acquired the skills to break into buildings and start cars without keys. Right now, he was far too thankful for those skills.

"Yeah, probably," the man rasped and loped off to the end of the dock and climbed aboard the cruiser.

He turned back. "Get that stock aboard, especially the cold medications," he growled and strode to the caravan.

A little boy, around seven of eight lay on a bed, his face pale while a woman held a bag high above him. "We don't have a gurney, but we can carry him," she said to Thomas who hovered just inside.

"Which boat?" The man nearby asked.

"The boat at the end. I've got one of the men hot-wiring it right now. Thomas is a more than adequate captain. He'll get you over there as quickly as possible and will arrange for transport to the hospital. The rest of your family is being sent to another boat, a fishing trawler. They should just about be on board by now."

The woman nodded. "Her mother, she's in the boat?"

"If she's one of the group... then yes. Do you need her?"

The woman closed her eyes. "Yes and no. Danny here should pull through, but I'd rather she didn't travel with us. She's... She's compromised—"

His mind blanked. Compromised. Shit! "Bitten?"

Her eyes widened even further. "What?" she squeaked. "Oh no, I mean she is too emotionally invested to be of assistance."

He slumped. "Oh, I thought you meant something else." The sweat that prickled his brow itched but he kept still. He needed to know more, so waited for her to explain.

"Sorry, I'm Cherie and my husband, Lance. Katie's our daughter and Danny's mum. There's also Lucy, her daughter. She tried to cover Danny but the men in uniforms... They had zombies on chains and threatened to let them loose if we didn't do what they wanted." She scrubbed at her eyes and the little boy moaned. "We have to get him to the hospital and get the bullet out."

Jack nodded and watched as Lance carefully scooped up the child in his arms, while Cherie kept hold of the bag of fluid and together, they climbed from the caravan and headed to the boat, Thomas trailing them.

*A*ddie fretted. It had been four days since Jack had left, with no word. Kelly popped by daily to see if she needed anything but staying close to home was what he'd requested. Instead, she worked in the garden, which had become overgrown. She snipped and cleared the weeds, choking roses, and used the rotary mower she found in the garage.

"Oh my god, what are you doing?" Kelly exclaimed, coming across her walking from one side of the yard to the other.

"The grass is too long and needs trimming. Besides, I could do with some exercise, since the babies I haven't been to a gym or walked!"

Clearly Kelly thought her mad. "But there's a mower in there."

Addie brushed sweat off her brow. "Sure, but how soon 'til we run out of petrol if we use it on gardens? Besides, I need to keep my mind active."

She burned under Kelly's keen observation. "I see. Well, I guess you've only been married less than a week and you still haven't heard anything, have you?"

She shook her head and waved Kelly into the shade, where she'd dragged an outdoor table and chair setting. "I found these in the shed too," she muttered, before dropping into a seat. "I miss him, and I'm so worried. I mean, I know he said four days, but this is killing me."

Kelly covered her hand. "He'll be back, Addie. He's resourceful, you know. I think it's kind of inbuilt into engineers. Before you know it, he'll be driving you nuts." She smiled.

"I don't know, Kelly. I mean it's dangerous. Anything could have happened." She'd always been strong and self-sufficient, and this sense of helplessness ate at her peace of mind.

"Just wait and see," Kelly muttered.

Once Kelly headed for home, Addie stood under the shower, washing her hair when a sound caught her attention from the front of the house. She snapped off the water and grabbed the robe, more than a little aware she was dripping water as she gripped the bat in her hand and inwardly cursing that she hadn't locked the doors.

Fiona and Leanne were in bouncers in the front room, she remembered, her heart catching in her throat. If it was a zombie...

Her moves turned swift as she hurried down the hall. If anything happened to them... Panic seized her, shaking her while her skin grew clammy.

She raised the bat then stilled.

A man staggered toward her, his clothes stinking of decay, his face worn. "Jack!"

She'd have launched herself into his arms, but he held out a hand. "I need a shower first, Addie."

Exhaustion hung from every word, and she frowned. "Get those clothes off and the water's hot. I'm just out of there."

He traipsed to the bathroom, shucking his clothes on the tiled floor. "They're only fit for rubbish." She silently agreed.

Reaching beyond him, she engaged the water and waited as he stepped inside. His shoulders hunched, she shucked her robe, then joined him. "Addie, I'm tired," he explained as her hands found his hair.

"I know. So, I'll wash your hair, then you go have a sleep. When you wake, I'll organize some food for us."

He didn't speak, only closed his eyes, and she poured a scoop of shampoo into his hair, created a lather then rinsed it. The soap she worked over his body gave her a chance to check for injuries, but other than a few bruises, he was fine, and she could at last breathe freely. "I... There's food in the car," he muttered, but it seemed that final piece of information exhausted him.

He barely allowed himself to be toweled dry before making to the bedroom and slumping down on the cushioned bed and fell asleep.

CHAPTER 16

*J*ack opened his eyes, and his stomach growled loudly. The stench he'd lived with for the last couple of days was absent and he felt rested.

Addie was settled on the bed beside him, and night had fallen during his slumber.

"Hi," she said, setting her book aside. He didn't know how she knew to put the book aside when he hadn't really moved, except she had some kind of internal radar.

"Hey yourself, beautiful." Her smile was dim and marred by a frown. "What's wrong?"

"Nothing's wrong, Jack. I missed you." She reached and touched his skin. "I was worried because you slept for hours."

His stomach growled again. "Sorry," he muttered.

"Well, it's good to know you're hungry. Maybe you should grab some clothing and join me in the kitchen. I've got a stew cooking."

"You found the provisions?"

She grinned. "Yeah. Fish and tinned goods? Yes, I did. And the other things in bags too."

She clearly hadn't looked in the boxes he'd brought home too. The baby items and the few other things he'd added along the way.

"Tell you what, I'll grab the boxes from the car while you serve dinner."

She opened her mouth, then closed it again. "I thought they must be work items."

Addie wasn't a peeker, he'd had to encourage her to explore the house and yard before she felt comfortable. It was yet another reason Jack had left the boxes in the car, sure she wouldn't be driven to check them out before he could explain.

The boxes weren't heavy, more cumbersome, so he ferried them to the front room while Addie went about her task, setting the table and serving the food.

The fourth box he put to one side and glanced at it one last time before joining her at the table. Two highchairs now graced the spots opposite, and he smiled seeing Fiona and Leanne bolstered and sitting in them. "When did this happen?'

"Tonight," she answered with a grin.

He kissed them on the head before settling beside Addie. Leaning in, he intended to kiss her, but his gut growled, and she giggled. "Food first. Passion next."

With a sigh, Jack picked up the spoon and inhaled, letting the scent of the fish dish envelop him. One taste was all it took for his hunger to flare. The food assuaged his hunger, and he sat back when the bowl was finished, replete. "That tasted so damned good, Addie."

"It's simple but tasty." She made to collect the bowls, but he stopped her actions.

"I missed you, wife."

His Addie's eyes widened, and her mouth settled into a sassy grin. "I think I missed you," she returned, eyes twinkling.

"Only think?"

Her grin deepened. "Hmm, I think I need a kiss to remind me."

He reached out, dragged her close and settled his mouth on hers. "Oh yeah, I know I missed you."

"Good," she muttered. "Because I didn't sleep a damn while you were away," she breathed against his lips. "I kind of got used to you being there beside me."

He cupped her cheek. "I don't plan on heading off again, to the mainland. Or at least, not unless I know something's changed and we regain control of the country,"

"Was it that bad?"

He winced. "Horrible, Addie. The creatures are everywhere and there're vehicles and…" Jack sighed. "You would have seen some of it when you came here."

"I stayed to the highways, and avoided every town I could. It was bad enough with all the wrecks and I saw more than one body trapped… or what was left. I never want to go through that again."

"Yeah." He agreed.

They sat for a moment in silence, before he nodded at the babies. "I've brought some things back for them."

Addie's eyes glowed. "Really?"

He nodded. "Can we take the girls to the lounge? Show me how to get them out of the chairs and—"

"They wheel, Jack. We just have to click off the brakes. I'll show you."

Rising together and leaving the dishes on the table, he followed her around and under instruction pressed on the tiny release at the back and with great care wheeled his precious charge to the next room where the boxes waited.

"So, you brought goodies?" Addie bounced with excitement.

"I sure did." He didn't tell her the contents of the fourth box were for them both. That would come last. Later.

He unboxed the items from the first crate, and she exclaimed at the baby play gyms, teething toys and soft animals. The second box, he explained, was full of items for older babies and the third toddler items and clothing. He'd also added a toilet training seat. "For when we need it."

Tears streamed down her cheeks. "Oh Jack. You're the best Daddy any little girl could have."

Her words filled him with pride. He'd been able to provide items they'd need in the middle of an apocalypse.

*P*utting the babies to bed, Addie soothed a hand over Fiona, who'd been a little fussy during the day. "Love you baby," she whispered before moving onto Leanne. "Love you too, sweetie."

Before turning out the light, she watched as Fiona fussed and scrunched up her face.

"Everything okay," Jack queried.

"I don't know. Fiona isn't settling well tonight," Addie whispered.

"Has she been like this long?" Jack frowned, and that made Addie even more concerned.

"She's been a little more fussy than usual. She's pulled at her ears and she's drooling a lot more than too."

"What does your book say?"

"My book? Oh! I didn't think to look. Let's go check."

Jack followed her to the lounge room and settled on the seat beside her. She reached into the baby bag and produced the book she considered her bible. "Umm drooling, ear pulling..."

Her face paled.

"What is it?"

"We should check her gums." Addie was up, walking as calmly as she could until she reached the nursery. Fiona was still awake, hand at her mouth, gnawing on her fingers.

Addie gently pulled her hand away and slid a finger over the baby's gums. "Oh! Wow. A lump."

"What's wrong? Do we need the doctor?" Fear laced his question, but Addie turned back, grinning.

"No. Our baby is growing her first tooth!"

"Her first... tooth?"

Her nod was rapid. "Yeah. She's not quite four months, but it's within the window. Might take a few more days, and we'll monitor it, but... Wow!"

He slumped against the wall, sliding a hand over his eyes. "Parenting, huh? Ups and downs and swings-arounds," he groaned.

"Jack?"

"Yeah?"

"Are you okay?" Her hand cupped his cheek, and he moved his out of the way, staring at her.

"I thought she'd stay a little baby a while longer. I've been enjoying them like this. Tiny."

"There's always time to do it again in the future."

His gaze turned hot and smoky. "Now that's an idea I like."

"We could practice?"

"No, I'd rather we try for the real thing." Then he frowned. "But maybe we should wait until she settles?"

"I have something that will help soothe her to sleep, now that we know the cause."

"You do?" Jack queried.

"Yes," Addie answered. "Down in the nappy bag. Before we left the hospital, as you know, they gave me lots of things. Trial packs and so on. There's a teething gel which will help her get comfortable and sleep."

His grin became wolfish. "Then let's go get it," and he hurried down the hall, returning moments later, holding out the bag.

Addie fished around, found the box and opened it, pulling out a tube. With quick moves she pierced the foil and slid some gel onto a finger and applied it to Fiona's swollen gum.

Within moments, it seemed the gel did its job and with Fiona finally asleep, Jack tugged Addie back to the lounge. "I brought another box home too."

"I saw that," and Addie grinned at him.

"You'll like the contents," he whispered.

"What?"

"Open it," he ordered, and she obeyed without question, reaching out and moving the flaps aside. On top was underwear. Sexy, racy and very, very lacey indeed. The matching panties nestled below. Then came pajamas of silky fabrics. Some simply exquisite and other pieces a little more explicit. "I hope you like it."

She blushed and held it close. "I'm thinking you want me to parade them for you?"

His eyes glowed. "I'd love you to."

Addie cleared her throat. "What else is in here?" She fished around and withdrew several packets of early pregnancy testing kits, raised an eyebrow. "Trying to suggest something?"

He blushed a little. "When you're ready, of course."

Inside her belly heat grew. Want and need coalescing into raging hunger. "I very much think we should try," and Addie couldn't help the husky sound of her voice.

"Only if you're ready. I mean, I know you're still breastfeeding, and the book said..." he cleared his throat.

"The book said what, Jack?" She leaned in, shucking her top and displaying the bra she'd worn on their wedding day, her nipples jutting erotically against the lace.

"That, umm..." His finger ran along the band at his neck. "You may not yet be uhhh..."

"Be fertile?"

Jack nodded. "Yeah."

"I read that. I checked in the last few days. I'm not using any contraceptive and we're not using condoms. I'd say every time we try is a chance and now, they're getting older and I'm planning on giving them some solids, there's a better than even chance that we might soon get lucky."

"Addie..."

His hands were at his waistband, and she couldn't miss the straining erection. "Is this making you hot, Jack?" she whispered.

"God, yes," he answered.

"Then we better do something about it, I guess."

"Get naked Addie... Strip for me."

Chapter Seventeen

Jack rose, his body rested and refreshed and looking down at Addie, a tumbled mass of warm woman with silky red hair, he couldn't contain his grin. Oh, the presents had done the job very well.

Indeed, she promised to wear one of her new ensembles for him today. Under her jeans and t-shirt.

The knowledge would tug at him all day, but now he knew exactly what he had to look forward to tonight.

She moaned and arched, still in the throes of sleep and he allowed himself a moment longer to study her before retreating to the kitchen. By the time the coffees were made, he was pretty sure she'd be awake. Jack carried the two hot drinks to the bedroom and settled them on his bedside table, remembering to use the coasters Addie had laid out for these occasions.

Addie groaned and turned and unable to help himself, he reached over, sliding his mouth against hers. "Morning sexy wife of mine."

Her eyes opened and for a moment he lost himself in the sleep hazed wonder of her eyes. "Hi," she responded.

"I brought you coffee."

She inhaled. "Smells great, but not as good as you." She dove into his embrace.

"I wish I could stay here, but I need to get into the office, make contact with Thomas and check on the new family and those who came to the island yesterday."

"You got the barge?"

He nodded. "Yeah. We need to empty the ship first. It's too big to bring up to the jetty so we're going to have to unload to boats and bring it over. Then we need to plan the bridge demolition."

He looked to the ceiling, aware that the safety of thousands lay on his shoulders. He alone could make the decisions and give the orders. If it didn't work, he'd put people at risk and made promises that he couldn't fulfill.

"It'll work Jack. It has to." Her hand slid over his shoulder, and he tensed then released the muscles with deliberation.

"I hope so, Addie. Things are getting grim on the bridge. Gus reckons one more attempt and they'll breach the defenses."

"What do you need me to do, then?"

"I want to bring everyone together. I need to arrange a community meeting. Not communicate via the regional reps."

"To talk about the bridge?" She screwed up her nose.

"No. To talk about the governance of the island."

Addie made an 'O' of understanding. "There's buses, right? We can get people here and..." Then she stilled, mind whirring over what he'd just said. "But why? I mean, you're making decisions already and taking on the role. Why do you need them to hear you?"

"Because once that bridge is gone, we're cut off. I've been making decisions for the last couple of weeks, but only because I inherited the situation, not because people had a choice and asked for me. Before I go further, I need to know I have their support."

"Then I'll organize it. Tell me when and where. I'll get in contact with them, or even better, I'll drive out and see the reps myself. You focus on the bridge, let me take some of the load off your shoulders."

God, his woman was amazing, Jack thought to himself. Strong and giving, supportive and understanding. After all, how many women would understand their husband heading off on a dangerous mission the day after their wedding, then on his return setting up a large event?

"You take my car. I'll look after the girls."

"After a feed, but I'm thinking, given their age, I should try expressing and leaving milk for them. Then if Kelly can come in and babysit, you and I can do what's needed from time to time."

He blinked. "I didn't think you wanted to. I mean..." Jack hated feeling flustered.

Her fingers slid through his hair. "The girls are nearly four months. They're going to start solids and there are potentially times when we need them to be cared for, so we can do the job we both accepted. It's not like I'm going to be working full time in the office, but there are times when this may be our best option."

"Only if you're sure."

She cocked her head. "That's what I love about you," she whispered. "You don't tell me what to do, and you don't simply accept the easy way because it makes your life cozy, but you check it works for me too. That makes you special."

◦◦◦◦◦

Jack sat in his office chair. If they made the run in two days' time, he'd only have tomorrow to make sure his calculations were correct. He could hit the bridge dead center, at the highest water point, and so long as they hit with enough pace at the right spot, she should go down quickly. In the meantime, so long as a fishing boat was waiting out of the way, he could transport Gus and the last of his security crew out of the danger zone.

Only, as an engineer, he had to be sure, more than a little aware they'd only have one chance at this option.

"It has to work," he whispered, the bridge designs unrolled on the table before him.

The rapping on the door broke his concentration and Thomas looked up. "Oh hey. You got a moment?"

Jack cleared his desk. "Sure."

"We have another problem with our plan," Thomas settled in the seat opposite him.

"What?"

"The Pride of McErin is too big. She won't go under the bridge, so the barge idea won't float."

"What?" His heart stopped beating in his chest for a moment. What else could possibly go wrong? "Didn't anyone think to check?"

"Well, you know, we were all pretty busy. We looked at the draught and the height by eye, and it's just, you know, not going to fit."

Jack's mind whirred. "By how much?"

Thomas grimaced. "Lots."

Jack rose and paced the length of his office, weaving his fingers together and pulling on the back of his head. "What the fuck do we do now?"

"Well, given Addie had the idea, we could ask her?" Thomas half joked.

Jack almost snarled, but his mind caught. The height of the decks, the size of the bow... What if...?

"We need to go for a drive, Thomas, but do you have any kinds of measurements?"

"Not unless they're on the vessel," Thomas muttered.

"We might not need that yet. Let's go."

He caught Addie as he left the office. We need go out. I've got an idea and will explain it when we get back."

"Okay, but Jack? I need to know, does next Monday suit for your public meeting?"

He grinned. "I think my calendar is clear, hun."

"Good. I'll get the information out to the regional organizers then. Set up the location and time."

He and Thomas walked out the door, and Jack took a moment to make sure it was locked then climbed into the car.

They drove in silence until reaching the bridge, Jack tossing over what he knew. The structure in the middle was the perfect point to ram the boat into.

"High tide is when?" he asked Thomas.

"In another hour or so," his friend answered.

Jack glanced at the ship, watching the men ferrying boxes of items. "We need to pick up the pace," he muttered.

"They're working as fast as they can."

"I need it empty by sundown tomorrow, Thomas. Things are grim over there," he nodded to the gates. "The sooner the better, Tom."

"I'll let them know. We can probably increase the workers on the boats and call in the rest of the fishers, get it done faster, but we're going to need to get the barge over to the pier. We haven't even started planning that yet."

"Use Lee's ship, hook the barge up and perhaps we can get the women unloading that. The heavy stuff can wait 'til we sort out the Pride of McErin."

Now he studied the boat properly, he noted how high the decks ran. Such a shame they'd be wrecking her, but necessary.

His mind settled to calculating. Set the boat so they hit the pylon below the waterline. He knew the Pride of McErin sported a bulbous bow, designed to decrease friction and to increase fuel efficiency—something he wasn't too concerned about right now. "We need to empty the tanks, so we don't have the possibility of a spill."

"I'll talk to the guys. They should know how to achieve that."

He grunted. PGH—the calculation of weight times gravity times height was the key to making this work, Jack thought. If we hit the bridge in its bottom half, we cause enough potential energy to cause the collapse of the bridge. Use enough force and the concrete will crack, and when weakened it would fail.

"I need a can of red spray-paint," he turned to Thomas.

"What?" Thomas' eyes nearly bugged out. "Why do you need that?"

"You'll see. I also need a harness. We've got them back at the depot, I think. We head back there and grab them, then I'm going to mark the bridge up. Who've you got lined up to work the controls?"

CHAPTER 17

*A*ddie looked at her list.

Finish the allocation of units.

Find housing for the new members.

Get the doctors sorted at work and find out what requirements for the kids were.

Take a census of the skills of the adults on the island, because surely there must be someone able to teach the children?

Deal with the influx of foodstuffs that Jack and his mission team had brought back. Find ways to protect their stocks and to hand them out in a fair and equitable manner.

Arrange the meeting.

She bit her lip. "Not much to do, is it Addie?" Only, it was. She needed help, because it was the blind leading the blind. She'd never before been in charge of these kinds of tasks, and she'd been winging it. But the responsibility... "It's not like I don't want it. I do, but I want to do this right."

Kelly would know who could help her. Likely Jack would be gone for a while. She cast her eyes about the office. He'd gone with Thomas in the police car, so she could use Jack's.

Making the decision she rugged up the babies, then carried them out to the car. Even as she made to climb in, she thought about Jack's reaction if he returned without her. He'd fret and worry.

The notepad in the door, and pencil had her smiling. He was such an organized person, usually.

Nipped out to see Kelly. Need a little help with some of the tasks. Will be back soon.

Addie.

She slid the message inside the gap between the door and the doorjamb, then used the keys she'd grabbed from his desk and started the car.

*J*ack returned, thinking he should let Addie know he was back and would be out in the depot then returning to the bridge.

He stopped at the door. Frowned.

Tried the lock and entered.

She wasn't there.

She hadn't left a note. The car was gone.

"Strange."

"Something wrong," enquired Thomas.

"Addie and the girls aren't here."

"Maybe she headed down to the market for some things. I know they're talking about how they're going to apportion the foodstuffs that have just come in."

Glancing around one more time, he shrugged. Perhaps she had. But a seed of disquiet planted itself in his mind.

"We need the spray paint you said and a harness." Thomas' urging had him turning away and heading for the door. He stopped, "just a moment," he muttered and wrote her a note.

Came back to grab some equipment but you weren't here. Come down to the bridge when you get this.

Love you

Jack

"We really need a more effective way to communicate," he muttered.

Thomas grunted his agreement, and they headed for the depot.

*A*ddie sighed, if only there were an easier way to do this. She'd left Fiona and Leanne fastened in their seats and ran up the short path before knocking on the doors, while keeping an eye on the babies in the car.

The door opened wide, and Kelly's father loomed. "Oh Addie. She's not here. She headed down to the beach. I can babysit the girls, if you want to go find her."

She didn't really know Kelly's father all that well, having only met him in the last few days, but she trusted her judgement and it said he'd protect them with his life.

"If you don't mind, Mr.—"

"Just call me Justin. Mr. Levine makes me sound like my father. He's been gone twenty years or more and was an unbending man. But come on, let's get those cuties inside, shall we?"

They ferried the babies and the bag of nappies inside. "They've not long fed, so they should doze off once they've played themselves to a standstill. Fiona's teething, so I've got teething gel in the bag."

Justin's hand folded around her elbow. "They'll be fine with me. Now go. She's on the beach brooding. I'm guessing about Thomas. They used to be an item; you know?"

Addie nodded her head. "I heard."

He sighed. "I'm glad her mother never knew they broke up. It would have broken her heart."

Addie wanted to ask what happened but closed her mouth. "Okay, well, if you're sure. I'll just head on down... the path over there?" He'd steered her to the door during their chat and now looked out, to see a rickety wooden fence, long stringy grass behind it and the tell-tale white sand.

"Yeah."

Addie marched forward.

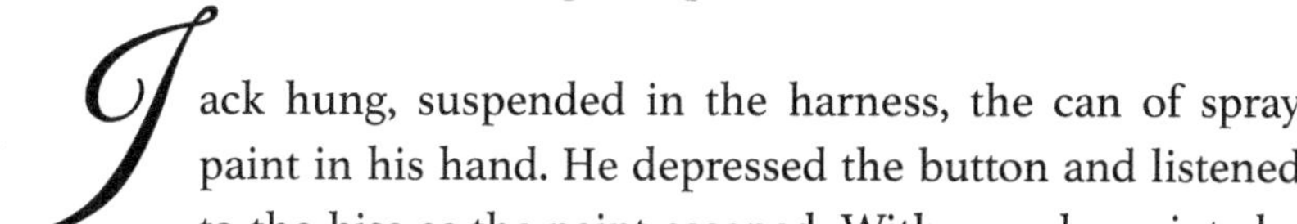

*J*ack hung, suspended in the harness, the can of spray paint in his hand. He depressed the button and listened to the hiss as the paint escaped. With care, he painted a very large arrow, pointing downwards at the pylon.

"They need to hit it hard, Tom," he called. "When it goes down, the bridge should simply collapse under its own weight. Our guys need to make sure they've abandoned the ship before it makes contact. We also need to make sure there's a boat ready for our guys on the other side."

Thomas hung over the side of the bridge and nodded. "You reckon the boat will sink?"

Jack glanced up. "We have to do this on high tide, so we have clearance on the bottom. I've looked up all the information we have on the depths, and I spoke with Micah, who brought the Pride of McErin across. It's only a matter of a meter or two, so we need to be spot on. There's no margin for error."

"What if it goes wrong?"

His gut clenched at that question. "I don't have a fallback position at this time," he answered. The admission cost him dearly. If this failed, he couldn't come up with another option to demolish the bridge.

"Jack? What do you mean you don't have a fallback?"

"There isn't one. We need to make this work. I need to create a plan. Work out how this will work. That's all I have Thomas." He started to pull himself up toward the top. He needed to see Addie. Talk to her. That would settle the agitation that was screaming inside him.

*A*ddie settled herself on the sand beside Kelly. "Hey, I was wondering if you're going to be busy for the next few days? I've got some ideas and I need help."

Kelly smiled. "Sure. Dad won't be helping with the bridge and unloading. He's not supposed to exert himself too much, because he had a heart attack before the virus took hold." Her face paled a little as she spoke.

"Oh, I'm sorry." Addie bit her lip, slid her hand down and prepared to rise. "I left the babies with him at the house. Is that too much? Should I go get—"

Reaching over, Kelly stopped her from getting up. "Nah, he's probably in his element with them. Sometimes he misses the interaction of kids. My sister Jane and her kids live in the USA and when the communication networks went down, he took it really hard."

She bit her lip. "I'm sorry about that. That would be hard not having contact."

Glancing at Kelly she noted the way her gaze took on a distant stare. "More for him. Jane's a lot older than me, and she'd already been married when Mum died. Dad's heart attack was in the car, while he was driving. She was a passenger, and it was horrible. He felt so guilty for ages afterwards. Jane came over with the kids, stayed a couple of months and he really enjoyed grandparenting, I guess."

"That would be hard. My sister, Celeste was a lot older too, and we lost track of her when I was young. Both my parents died from the virus. This stuff makes it really hard for everyone. I sometimes wish I had close friends or a mother figure, but life sucks, you know?"

Kelly smiled. "I do. So, what do you need my help with?"

"Lots!" Kelly laughed, and she blushed. "I love helping Jack, but there's too much for one person at the moment. Once they finish offloading the goods, they're going to need to be catalogued and stored. A system for distribution sorted. There's also the housing situation, I've got a public meeting to call—"

"And you're inundated as well as caring for your babies. Yeah. I'd love to help; it just depends on Dad. I want him to give up fishing but feel bad about even suggesting a break. This might give me the opportunity..." She rose and brushed sand of her backside. "And I'd love to call you friend, though I thought we were already on the way to that point."

Now Addie blushed. "I'd like that. To be friends."

"Come on then, friend, let's go get your babies and head to the office... Actually, dad would be happy to have them a little longer. If we just pop in and let him know, I'm sure he'd snap up the chance to care for the babies."

It only took a moment for Addie to see the benefits in that action. "So long as it's not an imposition—"

"I'll bet you he has them gurgling their little mouths off."

Addie laughed. "Okay then."

CHAPTER 18

*J*ack couldn't say why his nerves were frayed, but the longer he was gone, the more he felt uneasy.

"Now Jack, I know you want me to hit the pylon dead center, but ships and autopilots aren't infallible."

Jack grunted. "You've got to be precise. I can't guarantee it'll work if you don't."

All eyes followed him.

"Jack, calm down," Thomas urged.

He stood. "Something's wrong. I feel it."

Thomas stared at him. "Wrong?"

"I don't know where Addie is. She wasn't in the building, and I swung by home. She wasn't there either." His skin felt like it stretched tight across his shoulders as muscles tensed.

"Jack, she's a grown woman."

"With infant twins. A woman who's only been here a few weeks. She doesn't really know the island, let alone where to find help. What if something is wrong? What if I ignored a sign?"

At any other time, he'd have felt like he was overreacting, but not this time. His senses were screaming in his brain. He never ignored them, and he'd be damned if he would this time as well. Because if

Addie needed him— "I'm heading back to the office. We'll reconvene back here in an hour."

He scooped up his walkie talkie and hurried for the car, Thomas following him. "Alright, I'll take you. Keep your shirt on," Thomas growled.

They climbed into the car and drove in silence.

Once they reached the office, he saw the car, released a breath.

He used his swipe to access the building. "Hey, Addie?"

The building felt wrong. Empty. He searched the office spaces, bathrooms and out into the depot yard.

Silence.

No Addie.

He returned to the office and Thomas was frowning looking at a sheet of paper written in red. "Crayon?"

Thomas glanced at him. "No. Lipstick."

His gut curled. "Lipstick? What does it say?"

He didn't miss the glance from his friend or the worry and pity. "Thomas?" The word was hoarse, and he knew—or rather guessed— Addie was the subject of the missive.

"Jack..."

"Tell me, Thomas."

"She's been taken and Kelly too." The note was thrust into his hands.

He knew the spidery cursive. "Fucking Carl!" He snarled and read the words.

Jack,

You should have listened. Your plans will only result in our deaths, so I'm taking steps. Your woman and Kelly will fix it all. They seem nice. Shame they won't see the sunset.

"You know who wrote this," demanded Thomas.

"Yeah."

"We have to find them. Quickly."

"Get in the car, I'll direct you." They hurried from the building.

*A*ddie woke to stuffy darkness, an aching head and a confined space. "What the..."

Attempting to move her foot brought her up against a warm mass. Was it a... her mind blanked.

"*Urgh,*" a quiet moan warned her to be quiet and still. "Where am I?"

"Kelly?" She kept the whisper low, unsure where she was or how she'd got here. All Addie knew was they'd arrived at the office; she'd attempted to enter when Kelly screamed. Before she could turn everything had went dark.

"Addie, where are we?"

Her mind raced and ached by equal measure. "It feels like the boot of a car, Kelly. I think our best bet is to play dead until we work out where we are and why."

It was then she became aware of the movement and sounds of an engine. "I think we're turning, Kelly." A lock of hair draped in her face, and she tried to move it, only to discover her hands bound. "Fuck me," she whispered.

"What?"

"Are your hands tied Kelly. Whoever did this, I'm going to kick him black and blue."

"I saw the man but don't know him, Addie. But I'll hold him for you, then add a good swift kick in the balls to the effort."

Fury and terror bit deep. Fury that someone would harm them, when they were doing their best for the community. Terror because whoever had gone to these lengths didn't mean her and Kelly any good.

"I thought you knew everyone on the island," she whispered to Kelly attempting to control the black haze settling in her mind.

"I'm really bad with names and faces. Not really interested in being important. It's why I like working with Dad. I can pick and choose who I associate with. It's a small island, yes, but I'm a loner. I'd bet someone like Thomas or Jack would know pretty much everyone or at least have an idea who they are."

They turned again and Kelly and Addie rolled a little. "Fuck, Jack's going to blow when he sees these bruises on me." And there'd be a few, if the aches were any indication.

The car came to a stop, and she whispered, "close your eyes and be limp," to Kelly, and did the same herself.

The latch popped. "Still out, are you? I might have hit a little hard, but my pets won't mind all the much."

Something about his words had goosebumps rising all over her arms. *Pets?*

Hands gripped and lifted her, and it took every ounce of concentration to keep herself limp and keep her eyes closed. It was only when she was dumped on the ground that she was sure enough to crack open an eyelid. The building was dark. Damp and stinky, like machine oils.

Whoever dumped her had gone back, because Kelly slumped down beside her soon enough.

Hands unfastened her bonds, and Addie took a chance, scrambling to her feet while he was busy with Kelly. "Kelly, get up!" she screamed, and though her fingers and toes prickled and hurt, she was willing to try anything to get free.

The man held Kelly down and Addie jumped on his back. "Let her go, you sicko!"

He grunted and staggered, threw her off and Addie landed heavily.

Kelly must have taken up the fight because he grunted and fell beside her.

Addie scrabbled to her feet, kicked the man hard once in the guts and looked around for Kelly, who panted and cowered on the floor.

"Come on," she screamed.

She'd grabbed Kelly's hands when she heard that low dirge that froze her guts.

CHAPTER 19

Jack drove quickly, his head tossing over all the reasons he wanted to kill Carl. Apart from the pissy job he'd done as the regional coordinator, he'd messed with Addie. With their babies.

Beside him, Thomas was a cold statue of menace. "You're sure it's Carl?"

"Oh yeah. That writing is a dead giveaway. He thinks he's something special, and I'd just removed him from the role of regional coordinator."

"Timing."

He couldn't put his finger on any one aspect that roused his fears, apart from Carl's unwavering sense of importance, but the essence of his being screamed he should hurry, because Addie could very-well run out of time.

The car slowed, and he edged into the small cul-de-sac where the office of the regional coordinator was situated. The old employment business still decorated with, 'Come in today and walk out employed,' was a busy nest of movement.

He opened the door and several women glanced up. "I need to see Ellie."

The woman in question popped up, over the dark brown wood counter. "Oh, Jack! Hi!"

"Where's Carl?" He didn't have time for niceties, but she frowned at his harsh demand.

"Carl? I think he's at home. Stewing. Why?"

Jack thrust the paper at her, aware Thomas was watching closely.

"Well, fuck! I don't know. I mean, his house is nearby. I can take you there and we can see. Other than that..." She shrugged. "It's hard to know. He had a finger in lots of pies."

"Take us there," he demanded, and Ellie glanced over his shoulder, paled and nodded.

Thomas climbed into the driver's seat of the police car and Ellie scrambled into the back, Jack slamming the door with frustration. "Give me the directions."

It was only moments later, they pulled into the driveway of a pale bricked mausoleum, with arches painted in white, palms framing ornate fencing and an air of menace.

They pressed the button, and no one emerged. "Thomas?"

His friend sighed. "I didn't do this, okay?" He reached into a pocket and removed a metal pick, inserted it into the keyhole and moved it with cautious actions. The gate popped open, and they strode in. Jack contained the rage building inside him, though the containment was already wearing thin.

They called out, circled the house, and though both Jack and Thomas agreed it was likely empty, they entered. Searched high and low and only when on the other side of the gate did Jack utter a harsh, "Fuck. Where else could she be?"

"You said he had a family," Thomas murmured.

"The daughters. We'll go there next. Ellie?"

Once again with her directions the trip was quick. This time it was to a smaller family style home. They knocked, and a woman answered. "Hello? Oh, Ellie!"

Ellie pushed between Jack and Thomas. "Where's your father? Is he here?"

The woman's face clouded. "No. I haven't seen him since you took over. He was in a furious state, ranting and raving. You know how he is." Her brows knit together. "Has he done something?"

Jack opened his mouth, but Thomas stopped him with a shake of the head. "He's taken a hostage. We've already searched his home. We need to know where he'd take them as we hold great fears for their safety."

The woman's face scrunched up. "Oh no! I don't... Hang on, let me ask my sister."

The woman, he now knew to be Sam disappeared around the corner to return long moments later with her sister following.

"Hi, I'm Nina. Sam said you're looking for our father. That he's taken a hostage. I have an idea where he may be, but you'll need weapons."

Thomas' brow rose. "Weapons?"

She nodded slowly. "He threatened the girls if I said anything, so I didn't even tell Sam. I couldn't risk them. My husband was in the first wave and they're all I have left." Her voice broke at the end, tears tumbling down gaunt cheeks.

Jack understood her fears. He'd do anything to protect Addie and those babies too. "We know he's got a hidey-hole—"

"He's got zombies," Nina whispered.

His mind stopped, along with his heart. Three words that might destroy his entire world. *He's got zombies...*

Thomas grabbed his arm, offering support but it felt like the world retreated, went fuzzy around the edges.

They talked around him. "Addie," he got out past frozen lips.

"We'll find her, Jack. Nina's going to show us where we need to go."

He followed feeling so removed from the world and his mind filled with visions of faces, open mouths and the stench. Jack climbed into the car on autopilot. Thomas reached out. "Come on, Jack. I need you with me. Can you maintain?"

"I... Yeah," but the sound was a hoarse whisper. I'm coming Addie, his mind whispered to the universe. He only hoped they'd be in time.

*A*ddie panted, feeling the surge of adrenaline and searched the shed. "Come on, Kelly," she called and was rewarded by her friend clambering up and retreating to Addie's side.

The place stank, and she hoped that would assist in masking their location. She knew zombies had poor sight and even though their particular stink was extreme, they needed that sense to find their prey.

"Kelly, how good are you at climbing," she murmured.

"What?"

"In the market, I got up high, beyond their reach. The roof is the best place for us to go, but we need to climb."

Kelly stared. "How do we get up there?" She pointed to the walls. "There doesn't appear to be any easy way up."

But in a far corner, Addie spied an implement. "We need to reach the corner. I'm shit at throwing stuff, but I'm hoping with all the fishing you do, you might be better at it."

"Huh?"

"I need you to provide a distraction. Throw something so they head in another direction, and we can get to the corner. Past him." Addie pointed to the man curled in a fetal position on the floor, groaning.

"Shouldn't we, like, help him?"

Under normal circumstances Addie would agree, but he'd brought them here for his zombie 'pets' as he'd called them. "I... We need to get out. It's him or us, Kelly." Terror laced her words, but she remained resolute. There was only one chance for survival, and she'd take it.

"Okay." Kelly glided to the workbench, reached and tugged up an implement. "This spanner should make enough noise," she whispered.

Addie waited as Kelly drew back her arm and threw it with as much might as she could muster. It clanged on a metal wall then fell to the floor, the connection with the concrete making a deep bang.

Grabbing Kelly's arm, Addie towed her to the edge of the building. The ladder wasn't sturdy, but it was all they had. Addie held it still and urged Kelly up, before following as fast as she could.

The sound had caused the zombies to momentarily move in the direction of the spanner, but they heard the clatter of the ladder on the wall and sounds of exertion as the two women climbed. Addie reached down after swinging her body onto one of the rafters.

Her hand slipped, and she'd have fallen, but Kelly grabbed her. "What are you doing?"

With a grunt Addie tried again and this time the ladder swung up. "Help me up with this," she yelled.

Kelly, eyes wide assisted.

Addie dragged the belt from her jeans, muttering while Kelly held the metal implement against the rafter. "Good, hold it and I'll secure it."

Kelly watched then shook her head. "Whatever."

With the job completed, Addie hugged the rafter.

"Why did you do that?"

"At some point, they'll leave the building. When they do, we can get down, and hopefully escape. If the ladder falls though, we're stuck up here. If we jump it's so far, we'll hurt ourselves then we'll be even more stuck."

Kelly opened her mouth then closed it again. "When I grow up, I want to be able to think like you, Addie." She ended with a shaky laugh.

Truthfully, Addie thought, if they got out of here, she wanted to be the badass she was pretending to be. If only. Tears filled her eyes. Jack and the babies now at the forefront of her memories.

She just wanted to get home to them.

*H*is eyes widened on the old mechanics shop, set back in a ring of overgrown shrubs.

Someone called out, "Have pity," but it wasn't Addie's voice. He couldn't hear the babies either and hoped that didn't mean he was too late. God, let her and the girls be okay. I'll do anything, give anything. Just let them live.

His chest bellowed, as if he'd run a million miles.

He followed Thomas, Ellie and Nina to the fence. "It's locked," he muttered.

Thomas tugged out his implement again, working at the lock until it sprang free. A scream echoed in the air. Jack's hair stood on end as it went on, high and piercing then ended.

"Fuck," muttered Thomas. "Nina, Ellie! Get in the car. Lock it. Jack?"

He turned and caught his friend's gaze. Knew what he was asking. "If Addie's in there, we're going to get her out safely." He just hoped that was actually the case, not just him fooling himself.

He tugged the pistol out of the holster he wore, released the safety catch and followed Thomas along the overgrown path to the door.

"I'll open the door; you stay back in case they're near it." Jack followed Thomas' instructions.

The door opened with a groan and Jack waited for the 'all clear' from Thomas then peeked around the corner. Six zombies bent over... God, help the poor sod on the floor. He could only dimly make out a pair of feet on the ground, but he was sure it wasn't Addie. Vertigo hit for only a second, but he blinked it away.

His hand quested and found the light switch.

The zombies jerked, tugged away from their meal and Thomas moved in beside him. It took only a second to size up that Addie wasn't on the ground. He and Thomas fired. The bangs echoing. Two zombies fell while the rest advanced. His hands shook. Aim. Fire. Fuck, missed it. He aimed again, well-aware another fell and three continued to advance in their direction.

"Get back, Jack," Thomas growled.

Bang! Bang! This time his shot was successful, and another creature dropped. It wasn't dead but enough damage was done to disable it. With one still moving he fired. Between the eyes. It fell.

His guts warned him he'd be emptying his stomach pretty soon as the stench of rotten flesh filled his nostrils.

"Jack! Jack! Up here!"

He looked up and there was the most beautiful sight he'd ever seen. Addie along with Kelly, arms and legs wound around a beam.

He wanted to go to her, but the zombies on the ground needed to be dealt with first. "Keep... Keep holding on," he told her and watched Thomas finish one then another off.

"That's... Is that Carl?" Thomas questioned and Jack scanned the torn flesh that was all that remained.

"Yeah. Let's get the women down." He looked around but the scuffling sound above him had him jerking.

Addie was releasing a ladder and dropped it down.

CHAPTER 20

Addie's arms and legs felt like jelly, and they may have wobbled a bit as she climbed down the ladder into Jack's waiting arms.

"Oh, thank God, Addie. I thought I'd lost you, but where are the babies?"

She held tight for a second longer, needing the reassurance that this nightmare was done, her eyes scrunched up tight. "They're..." She gulped.

"They're with my father, Jack. Thanks for coming for us. You too Thomas."

Jack's arms around her, gave her back the sense of safety. "Let's get them out of here, Tom," Jack said, and she felt the rumble of his words against her face. It comforted and supported her.

The group left the building. "Jack, I need to stay here until others arrive. Nina and Ellie should make a statement and Addie as well. Kelly too."

Addie opened her eyes now and glanced at Thomas. He was pale, and seemed visibly affected by the sight of Kelly. She wondered if Kelly noticed it too. Jack released her only enough to take her hand and walked her out the door of the work area. Two women waited in the police car parked by the fence. She didn't know either one, but they craned and scurried to open the doors. "What happened?" One woman with grey streaked hair and gaunt features demanded.

Thomas stepped up to them as they made to enter the gated area. "I'm sorry to inform you, your father Carl is dead."

The woman's mouth dropped open then closed. She nodded. "It's probably better that way."

Addie didn't think that the knowledge of how he'd died, the sight and sound would help, so she kept her mouth closed. But the memory had her hand shaking in Jack's.

"Nina, Ellie, I need you to go with Jack. He'll drop you at the police station, then they'll send reinforcements but judging by what I see here, I'd say your father was controlling them."

The grizzled woman opened her mouth. "Keep it until you get to the station. Give your statement." Jack's quiet words stilled the woman, and she nodded. "Kelly, how did you get here?"

"It's a long story Jack. How about before we get any further, we head back, pick up the car and collect the girls? I'm sure Addie's anxious to see them."

She was, but she didn't want them anywhere near the situation. She'd do anything to shield them, she thought with resolve.

"Addie?"

"I want to change first," not because she was spattered, but because she felt grimy, inside and out.

"Kelly, you drive us to the office. Then head for home. We'll grab our car; Addie can change then we'll be over for the girls."

The trip was silent. The Sargent, a heavy-set man in his late fifties met them at the door. He ushered the two women in. "All right then?"

Jack moved in close to talk to the man, while Addie watched from within the confines of the backseat. He returned and climbed inside, Kelly turning the vehicle to the office. She only waited for the two of them to get into Jack's car before tearing off.

Addie watched the lights of the car retreating, in the gathering dusk. "I like her. She's got guts." It wasn't that she was avoiding the topic but needed time to compute and understand how everything had come about. The calm inside her hard won, and she gripped onto it. Let it bolster her until she could safely let go. Release the fears still roiling inside her.

Jack seemed to understand and drove her home. Once up the stairs and in the lounge, she started to divest herself of the clothing as she headed for the bathroom. Jack followed, she heard his footsteps and felt his presence. It calmed and centered her.

At the bathroom she turned on the water and climbed inside.

The water sluiced down her body and she felt the dam inside her failing. The terror of the last few hours suddenly rose to a crescendo, and she collapsed to the floor. Then Jack was there, fully clothed and taking her into his arms. "It's okay, Addie. We're all alive. Safe. I'll never let you get into that situation again." She cried harder.

"You... You can't promise that. People with their stupid fucking anger and their schemes. We nearly died because of him."

His arms tethered her in the moment. "Jack..." she whispered when the violent weeping passed.

"It's okay, Addie. Let it out."

She glanced up at his eyes, grateful for another day. "I love you, Jack. I spent all that time up on the beam thinking of ways to show you. I want to show you now but..."

"The girls?"

"Yeah," she groaned. "I just want all of us home."

A shadow slid over Jack's features. "I can't stay Addie. We're trying to get the boat cleared. I have to meet with the men."

She saw the conflict in his gaze. Her hand cupped his cheek. "We should dress, or I should. You change. Then we'll go get the girls. I can feed and settle them. When you're done, come home to me, Jack."

*A*n hour later, Jack walked down to the beach to meet with the knot of men waiting.

"Your wife, she's okay?" Gary enquired.

News moves fast, he thought to himself. "Shaken up but pleased the ordeal is over."

"You should be home with her," Gary offered.

"Soon. The sooner we finalize the plan, the earlier I can head on home."

He settled on the sand, shucking his shoes. "So, the Pride of McErin is empty?"

Gary nodded. "We finished about an hour ago. We found some hot dog sausages in the freezer along with buns. There's some in the basket over there for you to take home. We had an impromptu meal on the beach while waiting for news."

"Ah," he muttered. "Have you cleared the tanks?"

"There wasn't much left, I guess they planned to fill it up before the final run, so we actually didn't have to empty anything much. We've disengaged the barge and thought it might be worthwhile rigging it for tying up to on trips to the mainland. We can station it slightly off marina's and beaches. One thing we learned about offloading small boats on the water is stuff does get dropped."

"We lose much?"

"A bike and some dog toys."

Laughter bubbled up. Dog toys. Then his mind settled to dog, Addie said she'd always wanted a dog. The thought stayed with him as he gave instructions then listened to their plans. He wasn't a seaman. They knew what they were doing so in the end he nodded and rose. "Sounds like you have it in hand."

He plodded up to where the car waited and heading toward him was Thomas. "Just the man I wanted to talk to. That dog," he muttered.

"Mitzie? Yeah, I've got her in the lockup but we're going to need a home and—"

"I'll sort her out. Can you drop her over tomorrow evening? And if you see anyone, just act like you don't know anything."

Thomas stared, then a smile edged over his features. "The whole nine yards, huh?"

He grinned. "Something like that."

CHAPTER 21

Addie woke early and stretched. Feeling well and at least home. Her dreams hadn't been pleasant as memories of the abduction, trying to get away from the zombies and ultimately her captors' death at their hands had wracked her all night. Every time she'd woken, Jack had been there, holding her close. Murmuring it was over.

She rose but not before Jack's hand snaked out. "Okay, Addie?"

"Yeah. I need coffee."

His laugh was soft. "I'll get it. You dress. Today's a big day."

She didn't miss the concern on his features. "It's all under control, right? The bridge thing?"

"I certainly hope so. Otherwise, I'm not sure we're safe, even here."

Addie's heart ached with understanding. He carried so much responsibility. "I'm sure it'll be fine. The boat crew are experienced, you said. They know their job. They'll take that old bridge down and we'll be safe."

He sighed and scrubbed a hand over bleary eyes. "I hope so."

As she dressed, Addie considered the guilt he carried at what happened to her yesterday. She wished she could relieve him of it. The babies slept on, and she was grateful they were now sleeping for a good eight hours, having settled into a routine.

In the kitchen she found him on the floor, eyes closed though sitting up. "Jack?" A thread of worry echoing.

His eyes opened. "Yeah, just tired, Addie." He rose, and she moved in, winding her arms around his middle. "I know you've got to give your statement today to Thomas. I will be there, but I've got the—" He waved his hands.

"Thomas said he could take my statement tonight, so let's focus on one thing first, okay? What time is high tide?"

"Eleven forty," he muttered.

"What time do you need to be there, then? You'll want to talk to the crew before they board, I'm guessing."

"Yeah, I've got about an hour."

"Okay, let me pack the bag for the girls and me. You can get hats and sunscreen and water for us."

His mouth dropped open. "What?"

"We're coming with you. Whether it works or not, I'll always be there for you Jack."

He slumped. "Addie..."

"It won't fail, Jack. I have this feeling. I always trust them. It was one of those feelings that brought me here."

He laughed and tugged her close. "Then thank god for your feelings. Go. Get them ready if you insist."

Now she grinned, gave a sassy twist of her hips as she tugged away. "I do."

The roar of the boats engine chugging down the channel echoed and his hand held onto Addie, soaking up her reassurance.

His hat shading him, while the babies slept peacefully in the twin pram he'd found in a baby shop. The hastily erected sunshade keeping them from burning while he and Addie watched the Pride of McErin gather speed.

The small dinghy's they'd claimed would evacuate the men moments before impact dragging by the side of the ship.

With each second his heart rate increased.

"It'll be fine," she said. Others crowded around, watching the action, word having spread far and wide over the island. Another boat chugged the width of the channel heading to the edge of the bridge where his people waited. Gus has his men ready to abandon their post once the bridge failed.

If it failed.

His hands clenched.

"Oww," she whispered, and he blushed, releasing the death grip.

Men started down the side of the boat, he could barely make them out in the yellow high visibility vests he insisted they wear. One. Two. "Where the fuck is Gary?" He muttered.

The bridge loomed now. They'd have to cast off soon or it would be too late.

The timing essential to everyone's survival.

Three. He released the pent-up breath as the last man scurried down the side.

The rope flung in the air.

Silence on the beach broken only by the sound of engines screaming. They'd agreed last night Gary would set the boat to full throttle then abandon the ship.

The dinghy bounced and jumped.

The men hanging to the sides, then the engine started, and they motored away.

He held his breath.

Bang!

Crash!

A cracking sound filled the air.

The bridge swayed.

The boats engines screamed its revolt.

"Go down," he breathed.

It shook, a creaking and groaning then shattered pieces of concrete rained down as the bridge collapsed.

Screams and whoops filled the air, but all he could hear was the bridge disintegrating beneath the impact of the Pride of McErin.

"You did it, Jack! I knew you would."

Addies arms slid around him, and he watched for a second longer, then gave in to her embrace. "I didn't..." He slid his tongue over his dry lips. "I wasn't sure, Addie, but it worked."

She rose onto tiptoes, kissing him on the lips.

His world righted and his arms would around her. Keeping her warm body tight against his. *God, I wish we could go home now.*

The end of yesterday's saga though had to be played out. They were due to meet Thomas and the Sargent at the police station and he knew that couldn't be put off any longer.

They gathered the pram, the bag and babies then headed up to the roadside. His gaze taking in the sight. The island was peaceful. They'd found the nest of zombies and it appeared they'd successfully cleaned it out, the bridge was down. His people safe. More importantly, his family was safe.

Parking at the station, he helped Addie from the car, and they each gathered up a carrier. Thomas met them with a huge smile. "Demolition complete I see," he muttered and ushered them inside.

Unlike in the movies, they had to move past a small secure room at the front, a large grate pulled down and a swipe secured door opened to admit them to a large office area.

Thomas settled them in comfortable seats in an interview room and the Sargent joined them. "Good, you were able to come in, Addie and Jack."

He settled his bulk at the table, Thomas taking the spot at the end of the table. "We're going to record your interview. We want to be sure it's right. Now tell us in your words what happened.

Jack felt her hand tensing in his grip.

"Kelly and I met up down on the beach, her father had offered to look after Fiona and Leanne. She was coming back to the office to help me with some planning." Addie turned to him, and half smiled.

"I need some help and she wants to break away from fishing. Wants her dad to take time to rest, I guess."

Thomas almost jerked in his seat.

"If you need help, then it's best to ask. Kelly's reliable, It's a great idea."

She settled back down and sighed. "We'd left the babies with her father, she said he misses his grandchildren in the States, so we got to the office, I was going to take her with me and check the groupings I'd arranged for each building. I got out of the car and headed to the door. She must have seen him, because she called out to me. Before I could turn, he hit me. On the back of the head." She rubbed the lump he'd checked the night before. "We came to in the boot of a car. I could feel it turning and we decided it was best if we play dead." She winced and glanced at Jack. "Sorry."

His gut lurched. "You don't need to be sorry. You've done nothing wrong, Addie." With his thumb he made circles on the sensitive flesh of her wrist.

"I was thinking about the words, but yeah." She hitched her breath. "He stopped the car and carried us inside."

"We found his car at the side door, inside the fenced zone. The boot still open," Thomas offered.

"So that's why I didn't see it afterwards," she murmured and looked down at the metal tabletop. "I... Anyway, because we played possum, he undid the rope on my hands. He brought Kelly in and as soon as he finished with the rope I got up and hit him. He tried to fight, but with me and Kelly... we overpowered him." She shuddered and when he would have moved to comfort her, Addie shook her head.

"We threw a spanner once we knew there were zombies, and it occupied them. I saw the ladder, and we ran for it then climbed. We'd hurt him, so he was still on the floor. He..." Now tears shone in Addie's eyes and it broke him inside. "I caused him to die," she whispered.

The Sargent leaned forward. "None of that now, Addie. He planned for you two to suffer. It's not your fault."

But the tears streamed down her face and Jack moved, hunkering down beside her chair. "Addie, hun, it was him or you. He wouldn't have cried if you died, sweetheart but I'd have been broken and our babies wouldn't have their mother."

"But I—"

He stopped her words with a finger over her lips. "No. It's not your fault. Never could be."

Thomas passed tissues, and she wiped her face and blew her nose. "I'm sorry. I was trying so hard to hold it together."

Jack retreated to his chair and waited.

"You got up the ladder," prompted Thomas.

"We got onto the rafters, and I pulled the ladder up. Kelly asked me why and I explained that the zombies would eventually leave, and we'd have to be able to get down. That's when they turned, saw him on the floor and attacked. It was..." A pallor settled on her skin now and he could see beads of sweat gathering above her lip.

"Addie?"

"I'll be fine. I just, the screams. I closed my eyes and I think Kelly did too. But you could hear them. They were like animals. Then Thomas and Jack arrived."

He knew she didn't embellish the tale or add her emotions, but he knew there'd been terror. He'd held her last night while she sobbed.

"If he wasn't dead—"

"We'd have dealt with him, Jack. I don't have any more questions," the Sargent said and rose. "Addie, we appreciate your assistance. Jack, I've spoken with Ellie and Nina. Kelly also popped in last night, so we know the story of what occurred. His rage took it a step too far."

"At me?" He queried.

The Sargent turned. "At you, at life. His family, the world. He wasn't balanced in the last few weeks. Ellie only had part of the story. He'd terrorized Sam, Nina and the kids. Threatened to feed them to the zombies if they said anything. They were planning to leave, take their chances anywhere apart from here and away from Carl. When you stripped him of the Regional Coordinators role, it was the final straw."

"So, I should have seen—"

"Jack you couldn't have. You had so much on your plate with the loss of Lee, the bridge and Addie too. There's only so much one person can attend to. You were maxed out," Thomas said.

"Take your lovely wife and children home. Celebrate. Take a day off. Come back refreshed in time for the public meeting."

Addie's face fell. "Oh no! The meeting!"

Thomas grinned. "It's all in hand. I'm going to help Kelly arrange it for the day after tomorrow. Now go home and rest. Jack, I'll swing by later with the package you asked about."

Jack nearly cursed but Thomas smiled wide.

*A*ddie washed up from dinner. The girls had tried their first mashed pumpkin. She was now wearing as much as they'd eaten, Jack too. "I might go change," she said watching as he wiped grubby faces.

"Just wait a moment," he said and grinned.

"But..."

"Shhh." A knock came from the front.

On a huff, Addie walked over to see Thomas and Kelly carrying a large plastic box and several bags. "Oh, hi. Come on up." Self-consciously she tugged and shirt up then rolled her eyes, because pumpkin dotted it.

"Did we interrupt dinner," Thomas asked.

Kelly suppressed a snicker.

"The girls had pumpkin," she muttered.

"We can tell," added Kelly as she laid the bags she carried on the floor. "We brought you something from Jack."

Her eyes narrowed with interest. "But what..."

A yap echoed from the box, and she stilled. "A dog?" She turned to meet his grin.

"Well, I got it right, didn't I? You said a dog?"

Tears streamed again. Happy ones and she moved into his arms, meeting his kiss. "Thank you, Jack."

Thomas cleared his throat. "Her name is Mitzie, and she's available for adoption, if you'd like?"

Checking the girls were still in their highchair she tugged the little dog from the carrier. "Oh, she's adorable! Hello Mitzie. Welcome to your new life." Mitzie wagged her tail and yapped happily.

EPILOGUE

Kelly walked beside Thomas to the end of the pier, and they settled on the wooden slats at the end, feet hanging over the water. "I can't believe it's been three months already." She nodded to the remains of the boat, crushed by the hunks of concrete, the remains of the bridge.

"You asked me here, why?" Thomas' voice was hushed as if he felt the importance of their meeting.

"We need to clear the air between us, Tom. When we broke up—"

"It wasn't my idea," he added.

She glanced at the sea, wondering how to explain. "No. It was mine. I went to finish my last year at boarding school and while I was there something happened."

He waited, tension rippling from him.

Kelly bit her lip, felt the sting and the coppery tang of blood. She'd told so few people and it still felt like a great weight on her chest. But over the last few months, the urgency to explain had risen until she'd contacted him and asked to meet here tonight. In their special place. "I... I got news about your dad. About the fraud. He came to see me. Said he wanted me to talk to you, because you wouldn't listen. You were away at the police academy, and he thought

I'd have more success. But it was more than that. He... He made a pass at me. Kissed me and I was... It revolted me, Tom."

Now he may as well have been etched in stone. "You didn't tell me."

Tears burned in her eyes. "No. I felt dirty, Tom. I mean, it wasn't like *we had sex*, but I felt like I'd betrayed you. That's why..." She sighed, wondering if he could ever actually understand the emotional wasteland his father's actions had wrought.

"Kelly, if I'd known—"

"You didn't because I couldn't tell you. The nuns were great. I had counselling, and they helped me to understand it was your father, but back then? I couldn't face you. So, I came home at the end of the year and started fishing with Dad. He never once pushed me. Then he had the heart attack and... I just needed to explain, after all these years why. When Addie and I were attacked, it made me realise life is short. You have to embrace every opportunity."

"My father was a grub. But it's been seven years Kelly. Seven years of not knowing what I did wrong. Why you wouldn't have anything to do with me. Now you tell me this tale?"

She dug into her pocket and pulled out the letter from the police, closing the case. "It's not a tale. I felt unworthy and dirty." She shoved the paper into his hands. "When you're ready to talk rationally about what happened, come find me."

She stood and walked away, leaving him illuminated by the moonlight.

*A*ddie's hands fiddled with the wrapped item on the table. Wondering what he'd make of it.

He smiled and sat down, his hair still damp from the shower and his gaze settled on the tiny package. "For me?"

With a nervous bob of her head, Addie waited as he pulled at the ribbon.

It gave and fell away, and he unwrapped the paper. In his hands sat a tiny stick. Two red lines appeared to almost pulse.

Seconds passed. He looked from it to her. His face lit from within "Positive?" His words little more than a whisper. Addie nodded and he whooped. "I'm going to be a Daddy again?" His excitement filled the air.

"Yes."

"Well, I..." He pushed the chair away and pulled her close. "You're a marvel, wife. We should celebrate." Jack tugged away. "It's okay, right? We can still—"

Addie laughed. "We can and should. Oh, and your second present?"

Her hand moved to the bow at her waist and the silky material of her robe fell away revealing her nakedness.

His eyes gleamed, roamed over her body displayed for his pleasure. The heat had her body warming from within. "Let's not waste time then."

Hand shooting out, he grabbed her and swept her up into his arms, before carrying her to the bedroom, where he set her down on the floor before their bed. "If there's anything you don't or can't—"

She stilled his nervous chatter with a kiss, her hands working at the button of his jeans, her hand sliding within to find him already hot and hard. Ready.

"Love me, Jack."

With sure moves she slid his pants down, releasing him and jerked him so he fell to the bed with her. Addie couldn't contain her laugh of pleasure and his chest rumbled against hers so her nipples, already hard points of desire grazed against him. "Oh," she whispered as passion flared brightly between them.

"I will always love you, Addie." His mouth made a track from lips to jaw, then down her neck to her breasts. "I love your mind." He nipped. "The way you care." The nip this time found the other nipple, flicked it with his tongue. "Your body. All of you, Addie."

Then he captured her mouth again, his tongue sliding against hers while his hands roamed her body.

She felt him push the jeans from his legs and he stood, sliding his t-shirt over his head, so she could see every inch of the perfection of his body.

His hands found her thighs and parted them, his fingers slid across her exposed sex, and she quivered, already hungry for him.

As if he read her thoughts, he pulled her up, and slid deep within her, sheathing himself fully. "I love you, Addie. I love our daughters and I'll love this new baby too." Every word he punctuated with a slide and she moaned as fever gripped her.

"Jack," she crooned, her body on fire and the tension winding tight inside. "Please."

He moved slowly. Adoring her body with every thrust.

Taking her slowly as she cried out and writhed beneath him.

At the precipice, her eyes opened and all she could see was Jack. His face alight, eyes glowing with love.

"Let go, love. I'm with you."

One last move and she embraced the orgasm.

When she opened her eyes once more, Jack was slumped on the bed with her, arms wound around her waist. "Thank you for this life, Jack."

He smiled sleepily, "Always my pleasure, wife. Always my pleasure."

Did you enjoy this book by Imogene Nix?
There's more on the following pages. Just keep turning to see what else.

INHERITANCE OF THE BLOOD BY IMOGENE NIX

In the darkness evil waits...

As a young bride Kira was whisked away from everything and everyone she knew, including her new husband and became Christina, an operative of the Displaced Persons Unit.

As the danger grows she sees an opportunity to save her husband Vasya and sister Serina. But nothing is the same. Serina is grown up —married and pregnant.

Vasya too is older and darkly forbidding. Trusting Christina doesn't come easily until a catastrophic event takes place. Now, knowing the truth everything he thought he knew is changed. But at a very high cost.

The four must work together to defeat the Demon, Zuor and the stakes are higher than they imagined and all could be lost.

––––––––––––

The burning at the back of her neck warned she was being watched. A quick glance didn't clarify it. Instead, she turned around in time to see her mother's face, pale. "Mama?"

She took a step forward, but her grandfather snatched her wrist.

The grip was painful, and Kira stilled. "Let your parents talk."

She didn't know what the topic of conversation was, but it couldn't be good.

The dappled sunlight seemed cooler than before.

Her father crooked his forefinger at her grandfather while they stood there. For a moment she wished Vasya had come with them, but he had to work. Just the thought of her new husband warmed Kira.

She only had a few minutes to contemplate her newly defined status as a married woman, when her grandfather pulled at her hand. "Come with me." He tugged and, confused, Kira allowed herself to be towed away.

A glance at her parents' faces stole any feeling of well-being.

"Grandfather?"

"Shh, my love. You must go." His grip was implacable and his face stern, but he shivered.

"What are you doing? Where are you taking me, Grandfather?"

They moved rapidly through the village they'd visited to sell their wares just that morning, and for the first time since they'd arrived in the market place she felt fear. What was wrong? Was it something to do with Vasya?

"You are in danger. We must send you away." The words confused her further. Send her away? Danger?

"Where is Vasya?" She stumbled over a stone, but he kept tugging her onwards.

With a quick glance around, he hauled her into a dirty laneway between the buildings. Kira gasped, trying to drag air into her starving lungs. "There's no time. We must get you away."

A nondescript shopfront lay ahead, and he pushed on the door. It rattled and opened with a loud groan. "Andre? Andre, are you here?"

An older man shuffled into the room, bent nearly double from the weight of the load on his back. "Marat? What do you want?"

"My granddaughter. They are coming for her and us. Get her away. Take her now, while you can."

The man's face clouded over. "Are you sure?"

"Grandfather, where is Vasya?" Fright had the blood in her veins pounding.

"Hush, my precious. Andre will see you well." He turned. "Whatever it takes, Andre. Take her now." With surprising speed, her grandfather whirled and was gone.

The man, Andre, eyed her. "Come this way, child. There is no time to be lost."

Eleven years later

The tattoo of her heart and cry of terror woke her, as they usually did. Once again, as she had since that rapid flight from those who sought her, she found herself in a lonely bed. Hundreds of miles away from everything she'd dreamed of, in a house she'd built for them to share. As always, it left her wishing that Vasya had fled with her.

Instead, here she was, exiled without her husband. With a sob, she rolled over and let the tears fall.

Available from Beachwalk Press
books2read.com/IOTB

Direct Autographed Copy
http://bit.ly/2w6g4K6

THE CELTIC CUPID TRILOGY

When Cupid—otherwise known as Diocail— is banished from his home on a remote Scottish Island, he's set a series of tasks by the great god Lugh, who also happens to be his father.

In *Blame The Wine*, he must bring two lovers together... BBW Cara and James, the man she's lusted over from afar who happens to be a super geek and head Veha Industries.

In *A Stranger's Embrace*, Diocail is driven to help an emotionally fragile Jane and Davis, a famous author. The task is more complicated, with the existence of Carstairs her could-be ex-husband and teenage daughter, Frannie.

In **Revenge on Cupid**, Diocail must take the ultimate chance and find his own happily ever after with Simone. Sometimes the past gets in the way and HEA's don't come cheap though.

The dusty, dingy little diner was full, even with its current state of cleanliness—or lack thereof. People from the surrounding offices didn't care about anything except the incredible, well-prepared food at a reasonable cost. They flooded in, like waves to the shore. As one tide left, another swept in.

"Honestly, Simone. I'm going to try getting his attention one more time. If that doesn't work, I'm out of there. I mean, how long can I keep trying?" Cara picked at the caramel tart she hadn't been able to resist with the cheap metal fork and flicked the blob of fresh cream that sat on top to the side of the plate.

"You've said that tons of times before. Besides, what are you going to do to get his attention? Hmm? Walk naked through the typing pool?" Simone bobbed the straw in her smoothie as she eyed her friend with a frown. "It's been what? Eighteen months since you saw him, and you've mooned over him from a distance ever since you met him. You need to move on, Cara. That is, unless there's something you haven't shared?"

The query was arch. Cara shivered even as she shook her head. "No."

Simone quirked an eyebrow, obviously unconvinced with the answer. Cara let out a deep sigh of frustration. "There's a position...it's only temporary, for a PA reporting directly to him." She speared a forkful of tart, chewed quickly and swallowed, before continuing. "In his office, full-time for the period of the engagement. I saw the memo yesterday. I mean, I have the skills, right? I can type, answer phones, make coffee, file, greet people. What's more, I can probably do it better than all those size eights in the typing pool that Ms. Jackman seems to prefer." She nodded thoughtfully. "All I have to do is get past the ogre in Human Resources."

Simone stared at her, disbelief clear on her face. "Girl, I so remember that woman. If you think you can get past her, you're doing better than I ever did. That's why I left Veha Industries, remember? Maybe it's time to haul out your resumé and consider some other options. Look for something better." Simone shook her head and billows of her crimson hair swirled through the still air.

Cara understood Simone only had her best interests at heart. But this time she knew the outcome would be different. Hell, she could feel it in the air. The tingle of expectation.

"Cara, the HR ogre will hang you out for breakfast before she offers you anything like a position in that office. Remember her mantra? Good looks and good work make for a positive workplace!"

Simone didn't sugar-coat anything. It was another great reason for their long- term friendship. Honesty. But Cara didn't want to hear the truth in the statement. Even if it was exactly as her friend said.

Cara nodded quickly. "Yeah, I know, but if I don't try, then I won't know how close I can get to him, right? And the only way to catch his attention is to get past *her* and see him in person." Cara quaked a little at the information she needed to share. The favor she needed to ask. "Anyway, I tidied up my resumé and dropped the application into a memo envelope yesterday, so it's too late to back out now. I mean, fortune favors the brave. Doesn't it? If I don't snag an interview, I'm going to visit the career advisor across the street and register with them." She shrugged. "I'll look for temp work until something more long-term shows up. I can see what they have on offer and well…who knows? Maybe a job with the right boss is just waiting for me. But I'd rather this worked out, to be honest." Her voice trailed off into a whisper. "I really wish he would notice me."

Simone took a long slurp of her banana drink, and Cara noticed her questioning gaze even as she squirmed. Finally, Simone nodded. "It's your funeral. So anyway, you'd better show me this memo if you want me to be a referee for you. I'm guessing that's what you need, right? I'll have to know what I'm supposed to say about you before they ring."

Cara smiled. "Thanks, Simone. I knew I could count on you." She slipped a piece of paper out of her handbag and handed it over. "Sorry it's a bit creased. It was in the bottom of my bag, I stashed it so none of the others from the pool would see. You know how it is."

Available from Love Books Publishing
books2read.com/CelticCupid

Direct Autographed Copy
http://bit.ly/2vs7wtS

BIOCYBE BY IMOGENE NIX

Can a cyber-enhanced warrior and a ship's captain find love together?

Levia Endrado never wanted to be a warrior, but at seventeen she was deemed suitable for battle. After intense training and multiple enhancements, which gave her superior strength and healing ability, she was sent off to defeat the enemy—a killing machine with a mission.

When the war was over, she had to find a new life. At twenty-seven she's a washed-up veteran without a future. Or she was, until she met Sandon Daria.

Serving as a pilot aboard Sandon's spaceship the *Golden Echo* makes Levia long for a different and gentler life. But old hurts and even older enemies aren't so easily forgotten. Particularly when they come back for her.

Sandon is determined to show Levia that she's more than just a BioCybe...she's the woman who completes him. Getting close is just the first step, keeping her alive is an even bigger challenge, but one he's willing to take because the prize is their combined future.

———————————

Levia scanned the long line of other hopefuls entering the chamber. The large building in the center of town was cold, and she dragged her wrap around her body, even as she craned her head, looking to the high ceiling. She'd never before had an occasion to enter the testing complex, yet she'd seen the lines of teenagers every time they passed the building.

Once she'd asked her parents why the teens were lined up and her mother's face had shuttered. Her stepfather had just shaken his head and growled. They'd stopped her questions with a carefully uttered, "You'll know soon enough, Levia." The pain in her mother's eyes had been enough to shush her questions. For endless months afterward, her parents had traveled different routes to the educational facility she attended and Levia lost interest in the puzzle of that building.

Now, as she looked around, remembering that long ago spring day, it was her opportunity to find out. But she felt a surge of concern at what lay ahead. She likely wasn't the only one, given that there were probably two to three hundred seventeen-year-olds gathered in the one place. Ahead of her, she caught sight of a couple of girls, their arms linked together and wide smiles on their faces. Scanning the crowd, she became aware that, by far, a majority of those gathered displayed both fear and trepidation.

"All female subjects will enter through doors three, six, and seven. All male subjects will enter through gates four, eight, and ten." The speaker above her was loud, and she jumped before checking the numbers etched on the black metal sign over her head.

The massive doors beside her swung open, and now an uncertain silence reigned. Many of the youngsters hung back, clearly discomforted by whatever testing regime lay ahead. This was where they'd been told their futures would be determined.

"Oh gosh, I hope they only have an aptitude and psych eval. I don't think..." Levia turned to see the white face of the girl behind her. The girl had uttered what many must silently be thinking.

Levia dragged an unsteady breath in, her hand resting flat against the plane of her belly as she looked around. No one had entered yet. It was clear many were on the verge of taking the step, but still they hung back.

She straightened her shoulders. "I'm not afraid." It was always wiser to approach things head-on, she believed. When her biological father had died, she'd been one of the few to view his capsule before it was sent into the massive gray structure built to accommodate those who'd moved onto the next life realm.

Her legs shook as she wobbled toward the entrance. Beyond the doorway, she spied sealed cubicles and her heart stuttered. Why cubicles? Usually testing—med and psych—were in eval-units, hidden only by billowing white curtains. She glanced back, noting that others had taken the first step.

"Move along, subjects." Once again, the androgynous voice of the address system blared.

Of course, given it was her seventeenth anniversary of birth, she was technically considered an adult now.

She thought longingly of baby Rald and her half-sister, Elda, waiting at home for her to return, and the celebrations to be held that night. That made her smile. She would need to make them proud of her.

She entered a row and the tall Educational Specialist, the edu-specs as her peers laughingly called them, stopped her. "Present your credentials to the scanner."

She'd done this many times since the tiny implant had been slipped below the dermal layer of her skin at birth. The small unit in her wrist heated as her details were checked.

"Enter the first cubicle, Levia Endrado, and follow the instructions to complete your assessment."

Thus dismissed, Levia moved to the first unit, laid her palm against the scanner, and the door slid open soundlessly.

"Welcome, Levia Endrado. Take your place in the eval-unit." The soft contralto of the voice echoed after the door closed silently behind her.

"What are you evaluating?" Her voice was breathy, and she peered around.

"Your skills—physical and psychological. Your emotional and medical status. Your educational attainment levels."

It was an answer that shed little insight into the many things she was hungry to know. "Why do all seventeen year olds—"

"Take a seat, Levia. Then we may begin your testing."

If she'd expected an answer, she was sadly mistaken, she considered sourly. She dropped into the seat, the soft leather-like surface molding to her body.

"Levia Endrado, you are required to remove all non-specified apparel."

She jolted in the chair. "It's cold."

"The temperature will be amended. Remove the non-specified apparel."

Her misgivings grew as she dragged off the light wrap she'd brought with her, and then threw it to the floor at the side of the unit.

"We will begin, Levia Endrado. At any time, should you experience any malfunctions of the unit, simply depress the red button." It glowed and she grimaced.

Levia reclined against the chair and waited for the testing to begin.

The first examination was based on her understanding of the political system, where she saw herself, and her knowledge of the rights and responsibilities accorded through citizenship of both her planet and the commonwealth.

The second test was mathematical and scientific proficiency. It felt like hours had passed by the time she'd finished, and she lay limp on the seat, exhausted.

"Levia Endrado, you may rise. The sanitary unit will emerge once you trigger the yellow button at the door. Should you require refreshment, press the blue button and a restorative will be made available."

"Can I leave?"

"Negative, Levia Endrado. Your needs will be catered for in this capsule."

"Why?" Her voice hitched and true fear rose for the first time. Why did they keep her in the alcove?

"All will be revealed at the end of the testing cycle."

Levia looked at the now empty screen before hurling a curse word. It was met with silence.

The urgent throb of her bladder reminded her that she needed to use the facilities, so, with

a sigh, she rose and clambered from the seat. After attending to the needs of her body, she walked around the unit, peering at the door, but it was obviously programmed remotely. She poked and prodded, but it made no difference. With a huff, she headed back to the chair.

The moment she'd settled in, the viewing screen shone bright. "Welcome back, Levia. The next sequence will evaluate your psychological reflexes, then that will be followed up with the general knowledge portion of the evaluation."

"When can I leave?" It seemed better to ask bluntly, she told herself.

"Once the examination is completed. After the next set of evaluations, you will be subjected to the physical aspect."

"Then I can go home?"

"Levia Endrado, you will now complete the psychological test. This will be undertaken by one of the center's personal evaluators."

She frowned. Personal evaluators? She bit her lip, and the sting reminded her that this wasn't something to joke about. In her seventeen years, she'd only heard of personal evaluators being brought in once before, and that was when one of the girls at her academy had been in a serious accident. Both legs were amputated and her body's ability to keep her alive had been gravely compromised. Her peers had been informed that the girl had requested the assessment before she could request her support systems be disconnected.

"Levia Endrado, are you ready to recommence processing?" The emotionless voice echoed once more and she gulped.

"Yes."

Available from Beachwalk Press
http://www.beachwalkpress.com

Direct Autographed Books
http://bit.ly/BioCybe

ALSO BY IMOGENE NIX

<u>Warriors of the Elector</u>

- Star of Ishtar
- Starline
- Starfire
- Star of the Fleet
- Starburst
- The Star of Eternity

The Star of Ishtar & Starline - Print

Starfire & Star of the Fleet - Print

Starburst & The Star of Eternity - Print

The Secrets World:

<u>Blood Secrets</u>

- The Blood Bride
- The Illuminated Witch
- The Sorcerer's Touch

<u>House Secrets</u>

- As Dawn Breaks
- Immortal Consequences
- Unnamed Book III

All That Glitters - a House Secrets Novella (Coming in 2023)

<u>Danu's Secrets</u>

- The Downfall of Padraic O'Shaunessy (Coming in 2023)

- Unnamed Secrets Book II

The Automaton Series

- Haven House (Coming April 2022)
- Nobel Crest (Coming July 2022)

The Search Duology

- Miss Elspeth's Desire
- Miss Isabelle's Craving

Reunion Trilogy

- War's End
- The Assassin
- Executing Justice

The Reunion Trilogy in Paperback

Sex Love & Aliens

- Tangled Webs
- False Webs
- Covert Webs

21st Testing Protocol

- Cyborg: Redux
- Children Of A Greater Evil
- When Evil Came To Stay
- Finis: The War To End All Wars

Celtic Cupid Trilogy

- Blame The Wine

- A Stranger's Embrace
- Revenge On Cupid

The Celtic Cupid Trilogy in Paperback

Zombieology

- The Reset (re-releasing Feb 2022)
- I Dream of Zombies
- The Six Million Dollar Zombie
- Make Room For Zombies
- Unnamed Zombiology Book (coming 2023)

Knights of Pleasure - A Tantric Exploration Series

- Silken Knights (Coming in September 2022)

Single Titles

The Chocolate Affair (also in Print)

Falling In Love Again (Previously A Sapphire For Karina)

BioCybe (also in Print)

Hesparia's Tears (also in Print)

Tomorrow's Promise

A Bar In Paris (also in Print)

Inheritance Of The Blood (also in Print)

The Plan

Loving Memories (also in Print)

Hero of Heartbreak Hill (also in Print)

My One & Only

Curse Bound (coming 2021)

Raspberry Dreams (Not Yet Released)

<u>**Non Fiction**</u>

Self Publishing: Absolute Beginners Guide (With Suzi Love)

<u>**Written as Ciara Cave**</u>

25 Curated Ways To Get Rid Of Telemarketers

Book Signings for Absolute Beginners

ABOUT THE AUTHOR

Imogene is published in a range of romance genres including Paranormal, Science Fiction and Contemporary. She is mainly published in the UK and USA.

In 2010, Imogene Nix (the pen name not Imogene herself) was born. Imogene sat down and worked tirelessly for 3 months culminating in the book Starline, which became the first in a trilogy titled, "Warriors of the Elector." Since then she's had over 30 titles published and is now focusing on hybridising herself - with a mixture of traditionally published and self-published works.

In fact, she's taking control of many of her back catalogue books, which are slowly re-releasing as self-published titles.

Imogene is a member of a range of professional organisations world wide, and believes in the mantra of mentoring and paying it forward and is actively involved in mentorship (through NaNoWrimo and her vlog: In The Chair With Imogene Nix) and tutoring of new and upcoming authors.

In her spare time she loves to drink coffee, wine & eat chocolate and is parenting her spoiled dog and a ferocious cat along with her husband and 2 human daughters and looks forward to weekends away with her husband in their caravan "The Seven Year Hitch!" Do look forward to her caravan romance at some point!

To Contact Imogene

www.imogenenix.net
imogene@imogenenix.net

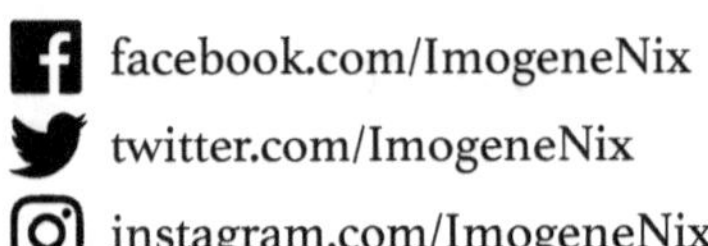

facebook.com/ImogeneNix

twitter.com/ImogeneNix

instagram.com/ImogeneNix